ROYAL REVERSAL

SHANELLE GOLDIENE

Royal Reversal
All Rights Reserved
November 1, 2021
Copyright © 2021 Understand, LLC
Author Photo Credit:
Steve Gabrail of Studio 41 Photography
shanellegoldiene@gmail.com

Printed in the United States of America
ISBN: 978-1-949511-36-9

ROYAL REVERSAL

SHANELLE GOLDIENE

PROLOGUE

The death of democracy was dawned not by the apple of discord, but by a single seed of doubt.

Doubt in the institution that promised freedom from persecution. Doubt in the legitimacy of the election of leaders. And doubt that the once great democracy could last longer than the Athenian democracy it descended from.

Scholars and experts alike had known and prophesied the end, but like Cassandra before them, no one listened. Chaos was on the horizon, as the people lost faith in the dwindling ideals of their long-forgotten Founding Fathers.

President Oliver Smith was not a very experienced candidate. This was something he hated to admit since he came from a long line of politicians. It was in his blood. His ancestor had campaigned and became "the people's champion" in the 1800s, when the Whyndam family came to power across the sea after the death of King George III's sons and their heirs, including the young Victoria. It was King Cassian I who took control of the British monarchy.

President Smith felt as though his family of politicians was just as important as the Whyndams were. The world had changed since, yet both distinguished families remained. His predecessor died of natural causes most inconveniently, and although President Smith had only been in office for three months, he knew that he could persuade Congress to approve his plans with the Whyndams. After all, there were no options left, and the money was running out.

There was civil unrest in an already divided nation, and the country's debt had skyrocketed into place values that even he had never counted to in primary school. The sickening realization was that he should have been paying more attention to the problems at home while he was vice president, instead of jet-setting across the world to foreign countries to be wined and dined by kings, queens, and other political dignitaries.

President Smith sipped his morning coffee and folded the corners of the newspaper page. He had always read his paper from back to front, as opposed to front to back. He always insisted that the media would throw anything they wanted on the front page to grab one's attention. But, if you read the newspaper backwards, then you would have more appreciation for the other stories that are more likely to be overshadowed by "big news."

By the time he had flipped to the front page, every maid, servant, and Secret Service member had been buzzing with news of the tragedy that struck from across the pond. President Smith had nearly spat out his coffee from the shock and horror of the article before him.

Yet, as he read onward, he hatched an idea that he assumed would solve all of his problems. He would make one last trip, accompanied by his dear family, across the sea. He was so sure of himself this time. The only hitch in his great plot to save his country was his rebellious son, but - even then - he was positive that this grand scheme of his would play out accordingly. Desperation breeds confidence in most unfortunate situations.

He stared back at the article once more, making sure he read every word correctly.

The English Enquirer

DAILY
Newspaper

THE
LATEST
NEWS

$2

VOLUME XI - NO. 27   Evening Edition   SPECIAL ISSUE

British Heir Alive After Attempted Assassination

Article Written by: Harold Bellman

Her Royal Highness, Adelaide Whyndam, Princess of Pembroke, is in fact alive and well, following her recent assassination attempt. According to the Enquirer's source, "The heir is in shock and has maintained a blow to the head while she fought off her assailant. She is recovering in a secret location." There has been no official statement from Pembroke Palace.

Their Majesties, King Cassian III and Queen Celine, have cancelled the annual Rose and Thistle Charity Ball to care for their only daughter and heir apparent. The event is postponed indefinitely at this time. This was a close call for the monarchy. Our most recent polls reveal that the princess should wed before another attempt is made upon the throne.

CHAPTER

I

Yesterday, they came for me. I closed my eyes, and everything happened all over again. Armed guards wielding their weapons, all pointed at me. My governess, Jacinta, screaming for me to run, as a guard threw a black bag over her head, covering her thick brown braids. Jacinta's husband, Giles, already on the ground, his face buried in the mud, his walking stick taken away from him.

My feet were already moving before my brain had time to process what was happening. I had outrun two of the guards at that point. The only obstacle standing in my way was the twelve-foot, wrought-iron gate that had fenced me inside the fields of the country estate for my entire life. The moment my hands touched the cold iron bars, they had caught up to me. I barely made it off the ground before they yanked on my fishtail braid, sending me crashing toward the ground.

When I'd woken, I was in a room I could have only imagined in fairytales. The walls were pearlescent blue, like the shining insides of an oyster. Gold filigree decorated the edges of the crown molding and even led up an intertwining vine-like design along the pillars of the canopy bed.

The bathroom was even more divine, which is where I currently was standing, gazing back at my reflection. The person staring back at me was a complete stranger, as I had never beheld myself in an actual mirror before. I had only ever seen glimpses of my face in the stillness of my bathwater.

I traced my heart-shaped face with my mud-caked fingertips. My eyes were what truly fascinated me though. Never having seen what color they were, I stepped closer until my forehead touched the smooth surface of the mirror. At first, I thought they were blue, perhaps picking up the cyan color of my cotton dress. But the more I stared back at my irises, they were lighter, like a kind of mist grey.

I was startled and stepped back from the mirror as the door to my room burst open. When I rounded the corner that led back into the posh bedroom, I flew into Jacinta's arms. She was the only motherly figure I had ever known. She and Giles were, for all intents and purposes, my parents. They have raised me and told me that my purpose in life would soon be revealed. Patience was a virtue that I had never mastered, but I waited, nonetheless.

I peeled back from her hug. "What is happening? Where are we? Is Giles all right?" I had a million questions.

Jacinta kissed my forehead and patted my shoulder. Two more figures walked into my room, flanked by four guards on each side of them. A larger middle-aged gentleman approached me with a familiar-looking woman, with auburn hair, to his side. They both shared my mist-colored eyes.

Jacinta stepped aside from me and curtsied low. "Your Majesties."

The man smiled down at me. Streaks of silver marred his dark blonde beard. "There is much to discuss." With the wave of his hand, he dismissed the guards. He and the middle-aged woman beside him sat on the bed, on either side of me. Jacinta sat down on the vanity chair across from us, quietly.

It was an uncomfortable staring contest. I finally spoke to break the silence. "I am not sure I understand why I am here or where exactly I am."

"You are at Pembroke Palace." The woman said to me. She grasped my hands on her own.

"As in *the Pembroke Palace*? Like where the King and Queen of the United Kingdom live, Pembroke Palace?" I asked.

Jacinta cleared her throat. "Dahlia, my flower. I never told you the real reason you grew up in the country estate. I told you that one day, you would be told everything that you had questions about. Well, that day has finally come."

I looked at everyone surrounding me. I would have thought that this moment would have made more sense to me. I had a whole journal full of questions I needed answers to. I wish I had brought it with me.

The woman holding my hands glared at Jacinta. "Is 'Dahlia' a nickname? Please tell me she knows the name *I* gave her." Her expression was filled with worry as she exchanged a look with the man beside me.

"My name is Adalia. Yes, it is a nickname for the flowers I liked to pick beside the gate as a child. Just like how Jacinta's name means Hyacinth, mine is like a flower too."

"No. Your name means 'noble'. It is given to children who have noble blood in them." The woman said.

The gentleman chuckled whole-heartedly. "Yours is exceedingly noble! Tell her, Celine."

Celine gripped my hands even tighter. "I truly wish that we could have met under different circumstances, my dear. I am the queen, and beside you is King Cassian III. I am sure that you must have seen or heard about us in your history lessons."

I nodded, unsure of where this was going.

"Your purpose in life is very special. Although it is the best kept secret in the world. You are our daughter, Adalia."

I took my hands out of her grasp. It was as if the entire world stopped spinning. My heart skipped a beat. I shook my head. "No, that cannot be right." This was a joke. A prank. There would be cameras popping out of the walls and a team of people laughing. At least, that is how I imagined it in my mind. No such thing occurred.

Everyone in the room looked upset.

"Adalia, you really are royalty." Jacinta spoke softly, as if telling someone that they were a princess was an everyday conversation. "They entrusted me with your care from the moment you were born. Mr. Lockwood and I raised you for this moment."

"What moment would that be? You always told me that I would find out sooner or later. How did you not know when that would be?" I put my head in my hands, trying to calm down.

A reassuring hand patted my back. Queen Celine said, "Mrs. Lockwood did not know when we would need you, if at all. Nobody could calculate how long it would take for your sister, Adelaide, to be assassinated."

A chill crept up my spine. "You are really trying to tell me that I am a princess."

"No. We are all trying to inform you that you are *the* princess of the British monarchy. In fact, you are the *only* heir now."

I picked up my head. "I do not understand. Why was I not told before? How could I not have known?" I shrugged off the hand that was on my back. I did not want to be anywhere near these people. How could my own parents not raise me? How could they send their daughter away to live in the country?

The king stood up and paced the room. It seemed like a nervous habit.

That was when I realized that I had been planning on doing the same exact thing. Some behaviors are learned. Others are … *inherited*.

I turned to Queen Celine beside me. Her eyes were red and puffy, as if she had been crying. Her eyes, though … they were the same as mine.

King Cassian stopped and faced us. "Your mother, Celine, bore twins. Our family had been receiving many death threats at the time. The world was a much different place eighteen years ago."

"I am only 17," I said matter-of-factly.

"Not for long. Yours and Adelaide's birthday is in a few months. Although she will always be

17, you will not. There were only a few select members of our staff who knew that the queen had twin girls who survived. The rest of the world does not know of your existence. Outside of this room, only three others know who you are."

Jacinta chimed in, "Giles, being one of them."

"So, what is my grand purpose in all of this? Am I to be introduced to the world as Adalia, your other daughter?" I asked curiously.

"No, my dear. Adalia does not exist. You never technically existed, and nobody knows who you are." The king made his way back to us from the other side of the room. "From here on out, you are Adelaide Rosalind Isadora Elita Whyndam, Princess and Heir Apparent to the English throne."

I gulped, letting that all sink in. I could not be a princess. I would not even know where to begin! My heart fluttered wildly. My palms were sweaty. For a moment, I thought I was going to pass out.

"I understand that this is a lot to take in. This is not easy for any of us."

I looked at Queen Celine in fury. "None of

you have any idea what it is like to wake up wondering why you are here, alone in this world, knowing that you have a purpose but not knowing what that purpose is, wondering what happened to your parents this entire time! Now, I finally found out, and ... and you do not love me at all."

"That is not true. We have been checking up on you all of these years."

"Checking up on me? What kind of parent checks up on their child? You both should have been there for me! I needed you then, not now. Now that I am nearly an adult!" I selfishly spat back the words at them.

King Cassian rose his sausage-like index finger in my face. I swiped it aside and ran to Jacinta. I knelt down on the floor beside her like a child who hides behind their parents when they're unsure of something. She wrapped her arms around me, trying to shush me.

The king raised his voice. "You have one month to pull yourself together, girl. Mrs. Lockwood will see to your education and prepare you to fill your sister's shoes."

Queen Celine rose from the side of the bed

elegantly. "What is happening in a month, my love? Surely, she will not be prepared by then. Have we not seen to it, that the Rose and Thistle event is cancelled this year?" She moved over to her husband's side.

"The Americans are visiting. President Smith and his family will arrive by then. Luckily for us, their son Aiden will not have seen her for years. They will not have remembered Adelaide or suspect anything different about her."

"Surely you can reschedule…"

"No! Smith and I have pertinent dealings of state that we must attend to. She will be ready by then to greet their son accordingly," the king replied hastily. "As far as anyone knows, Adelaide will recover from her assassination attempt in the West Wing. If the Americans—or any other guests whom we encounter—seem to think that something is amiss, then the official story will be that she hit her head while fighting off her assailant before the guards intervened and protected her. Amnesia is a delicate matter … one that we will use to our advantage." With that, King Cassian made his leave, followed by his queen.

Tears streamed down my cheeks. Jacinta squeezed me tightly. "Let it all out, flower. Shh ... shh." She brushed my hair with her hand slowly as I wept.

When I had cried my eyes dry, I looked up at Jacinta and asked, "How can I possibly learn to become a princess in only one month, when my sister trained her whole life for this?"

She did not have an answer for me.

CHAPTER
II

In the morning, four very cheerful girls came to wake me up. They introduced themselves as my lady's maids. They seemed to have a curious habit of asking what happened to me. Seeing as I did not even remember the whole story that the king told me, I thought it best to give them curt, to-the-point, vague responses.

This did not seem to please the maids, especially Constance, who I assumed was head-maid, as she gave orders to the others. They each had their own duty, it seemed, to help me begin my day. I could not imagine how my sister put up with this. It was utterly ridiculous being coddled. I mean, who cannot dress themselves in the morning or wash their hands?

Adelaide had clearly been living a very different life than me. I was lost in my own thoughts as Faith, the maid beside me, asked me all sorts of questions. She was too bubbly this morning for me to handle.

I barely acknowledged the other two, Grace and Verity. They hardly said a word and never even looked me in the eye. I decided I liked them best. At least they had the decency not to ignore my wishes. I made it obvious in my responses that I was not up for being bombarded by questions that I honestly did not have the correct answers to.

They exchanged glances with one another, and I even heard Faith whisper to Verity, "She sure has changed for the worse, I think. She is even ruder than before."

I do not believe she thought I could hear her, but it hurt all the same. If I could not win over my lady's maids, how was I supposed to win over an entire country?

After they laced me up in a simple cream cotton gown that hit right below my knees, something they called a day dress, I made my way to the door.

"Your Highness, you must be escorted down to breakfast." Constance said politely.

I put a hand to my forehead.

All of my maids rushed toward me.

"Does Your Highness not feel well? Shall we fetch the doctor for you?"

My hand fell to my side as I shook my head,

"No, there is no need." I must learn this protocol. "Who is supposed to walk me down to breakfast?" I asked.

Constance, Grace, Faith, and Verity all looked at one another.

They had no idea either. Perfect.

I opened the door and stood back, startled at the sight of a tall guard. He was dressed in the crimson and black uniform. The same clothing worn by the ones that brought me to the palace by force.

His striking aquamarine eyes roved over me as he stood a little straighter. He never moved his original stance. Staring straight into the hallway, he said, "My lady, shall I be of assistance to you?"

He was not like the other guards, I decided. Upon a closer look, his ink-black hair curled right below his ear. The other guards all shared short, cropped hairstyles, but not this one. His uniform was untucked and disheveled, as well.

Perhaps the palace was working this one so hard that he didn't have enough time for a haircut.

I looked at his nametag. "Yes, Officer…" I moved to stand in front of him, so I could read his name. "Officer Durant. Apparently, I need an escort to assist me with walking to breakfast."

My four maids shared a wide-eyed expression. Verity spoke up. This was the first time I had even heard her speak. "Your Highness, it is not proper for your guard to walk with you." Her voice was as gentle as honey.

"Then, will one of you escort me?" I asked them.

Verity shook her head again. "We are not meant to be in the open corridors and hallways. We have our own way of navigating the palace. It is not right for us to be seen."

"And, what of Officer Durant? Can he walk the hallways?"

He broke his stance and turned towards me, offering his arm. "I can, my lady. Shall we?"

My maids curtsied and closed the door to my room.

I looped my arm around Officer Durant's, and we made our way down the hall. Neither of us spoke for the first few minutes. We just seemed to keep walking in circles endlessly.

"Forgive me, my lady, but the Great Hall is this way." He shifted us so we could turn in the opposite direction from where I was trying to lead us to.

"Of course."

I was so nervous about slipping up that I could not even think straight. I did not know where anything was in this palace. Adelaide was supposed to have lived here her entire life. She was supposed to know where she was going. She was supposed to know that she could only leave her rooms by escort … or maybe that one was new. Even my maids did not seem to know who would walk with me everywhere. Maybe they were not supposed to know, probably because of what happened to her … to *me*. Ugh, this was so confusing! How was I supposed to pretend to be someone whom I wasn't?

My facial expression must have been a sight to see. I was drowning in my own mental turmoil.

"My lady, are you all right? You look as if you

might faint." Officer Durant stepped in front of me. Those blue-green eyes of his stared into mine, and for the first time, I felt like someone was seeing *me*, instead of the princess I was clearly failing at pretending to be. He genuinely was concerned.

"I am fine. Thank you. I have not eaten anything in some time, and I am sure that I just need breakfast."

We continued to walk—although this time, I allowed him to lead.

"It is all right, my lady. I know every inch of Pembroke. You are in safe hands."

I dipped my head in response, acknowledging his statement.

The hallways were so dark and dreary. All the thick velvet drapes were pulled shut from the windows. The only lights were from torches along the wall. It must have been ten in the morning, but it seemed more like ten at night. Then again, I was not supposed to be seen by the public. I was supposed to be recovering. We stopped in front of an extensive set of wooden doors. Two guards were stationed on each side, dressed similarly to Officer Durant. They stared straight ahead, only addressing me formally, "Your Highness."

I wriggled my arm free from Officer Durant. He bowed, turning on his heel as the other two guards opened the doors to the Great Hall for me.

With a name such as Great Hall, I guess I was expecting more. There were six long tables that would probably house fifty people on each side. There were stained glass windows, but other than that, there were no decorations or detail on the furniture. It was a large, plain banquet hall.

At the front of the room was a smaller table aligned with regal looking chairs. Each of the chairs varied in size and length of the backs. I assumed that the grandest in the middle was King Cassian's. The one on his right was slightly shorter and was most likely Queen Celine's. This meant that the smallest of the three must've been Adelaide's, which was now mine.

I sat down as members of the staff placed silverware and three kinds of glassware down. One even draped my lap with a napkin while another scooched my chair closer to the table.

The gentleman staff member with white gloves poured me some water and asked, "Should I send up the usual for you, Your Highness?"

I nodded, grateful that I did not have to eat with the king and queen after what happened yesterday. I was content in my silence.

Adelaide's 'usual' was a side of blueberry lemon scones and Earl Grey tea. The butler eyed me as I poured a dash of milk and used the tongs to fish out four cubes of sugar for my tea.

"Is there something wrong, er … forgive me, but I do not know your name. I mean, I do not remember it—after the accident, of course."

The butler bowed with one gloved hand behind his back. "Pardon me, but you mean the attempt on your life. From what we have heard downstairs in the servants' quarters, it was no accident." He took away the other two pieces of glassware. "My name is Zachariah, Your Highness. Forgive me, but we are not accustomed to speaking with one such as yourself."

"Oh," I said and grabbed another sugar cube for my tea. "Well, thank you for bringing up my breakfast. Might you also bring two poached eggs and another scone for me?"

Zachariah nodded and bowed before leaving to fetch the items. He passed another staff member and said in a hushed voice, "Not herself ... I'm grabbing more food."

The other boy snickered. With nobody else in the entire hall, I could clearly hear them. Was Adelaide deaf? Is this how everyone around her always acted, whispering about, talking about her behind her back when they thought nobody was listening? I was also tired of being treated like I didn't exist and having to ignore what was being said about me. It was obvious that the king and queen were telling the truth. Nobody knew that I was not Adelaide—even though I was not behaving like she normally would.

While the one who laughed about Zachariah's comment poured me more tea, I told him what I was thinking, "I happen to think that wanting a sturdier breakfast for myself is hilarious too." His face showed pure shock.

"I am very sorry, Your Highness. What are

you going to do?" he asked, absolutely terrified.

What was I going to do? I was not going to do anything. I just wanted to make it known that I was not deaf around here.

"Nothing. You may leave." I picked up my teacup and inhaled the floral notes of the lavender and bergamot scent of my tea.

The poor boy backed up into one of the long tables, spilling some hot water onto himself. He dabbed at his wrist before hurrying back to the kitchens.

A few minutes later, Zachariah returned with my food and a stony look about him. Clearly, he was told about what I had said. Good. Perhaps now they will refrain from saying mean things behind other people's backs.

~

After such a late breakfast, I skipped lunch and spent the greater part of the afternoon exploring. My maids were going to be furious with me if they knew I was unattended, but I did not care. They themselves told me they never were seen in the hallways. How were they going to know? Being a so-called princess, I assumed I could go wherever I pleased. I could not have been more wrong.

I was not allowed inside certain rooms. The guards told me that I had no business with the king, so even though I was their princess, I was not permitted to enter certain places. I was technically not supposed to leave the West Wing—except for when I was to eat in the Great Hall.

Eventually, my explorations of the palace were halted entirely. I had my dinner sent to my room, instead of eating another lonely meal by myself.

I caught whispers of the guards indicating that the king and queen were attending to urgent matters and eating separately. I saw glimpses of servants running around and heard the sound of shuffling feet, and the echoes of closing doors made me realize there was a maze of unknown passageways that the staff must have been using to travel from one part of the palace to the other.

After walking around aimlessly in the West Wing for a few hours, I settled back in my room. There was a different officer stationed outside this time. What did I expect? The same guard cannot have the same shifts throughout the day. I was disappointed all the same. It would have been nice to talk to someone. Everyone else just whispered about me behind my back or did not even glance in my direction. It was like they were all trying to act invisible. Maybe that was the way things were supposed to be.

Once inside my room, I peeked out of the entryway that led to the balcony. Outside, the air was still warm. In the courtyard below were a maze of overgrown hedges and rose bushes intertwined with scenic benches and ponds, with lotus flowers and lily pads floating on top. The evening air smelled of jasmine and gardenia. It reminded me of home in the country.

Tears welled up in my eyes as I went back inside. I drew myself a bath and let myself be sad. I cried in the tub until I did not have anymore tears left. I wept for the life that was stolen from me. For the childhood that I was robbed of. For the life I did not want but must now endure. It was maddening.

My maids knocked on the bathroom door.

"I will be out in a moment," I replied. Exiting the bathtub, I wrapped my hair and body in two luxuriously plush towels and stepped into the bedroom. I wiped tears from my swollen, red eyes. My maids helped me into my flimsy lavender nightgown and braided my wet hair. On the verge of crying again, I dismissed my maids for the rest of the evening. Each of them curtsied.

"Goodnight, Your Highness. We will see you in the morning. Sleep well." Constance was the only one who spoke for everyone, it seemed. I suppose that was part of her job as the head maid.

Once they disappeared behind the door next to the wardrobe, hidden behind a tapestry, I wrapped my dove grey robe around me and stepped out onto the balcony. I needed to get out of the palace. I wanted to be down below in the gardens. I was suffocating like a bird in a gilded cage, longing to break free. At this point, my thought process was very irrational. I was going to have a panic attack if I stayed in my room any longer. Fear and anxiety rushed through my veins. My heart sped up. I leaned over the edge of the balcony. There were vines and ivy crawling up the side of the stone walls. I gazed down below and was caught by a pair of blue-green eyes staring back at me.

The guard beneath my balcony stopped patrolling the gardens and shoved his spear-like staff into the ground and saluted me. "My lady, please tell me you're not about to do what I think you're about to do, are you?" said Officer Durant.

I put my leg over the side of the railing, my nightgown inching up my thigh. I whipped the other leg over cautiously until I sat perched atop the railing. I even swung my feet back and forth. "That depends on what you think I was about to do."

"It is not safe to be out in the open like this. There is a reason we patrol the gardens at night."

"Ah, yes, Officer. Should there not be more of you in the gardens? Especially when my balcony overlooks them?" I asked, squeezing my eyes shut as I sniffled from crying not too long ago.

Officer Durant grabbed his staff and walked towards the ivy-covered wall. "My lady, I must advise you to go back inside your room."

I shook my head. "I will, in a moment."

"No, it is not safe for you." He demanded.

"You said that already." I was almost hyperventilating now. I knew I was going to explode with more tears. "Go away!" I yelled at him.

Instead of backing away, to my surprise, he began climbing up the vines. I guess they were sturdier than I suspected. I leaped off the edge of the balcony railing and backed away as he climbed over. There was very little room for the two of us on my balcony space together.

"You could have gotten yourself killed. What were you thinking?" I chastised him.

Officer Durant chuckled. "I am only trying to ensure your safety, princess." The way he said my title was almost as if he were cursing me. "You must have really hit your head, because I've been told that you are severely afraid of heights."

Heat rose to my cheeks as the wind picked up,

rustling my robe and nightgown. The way this arrogant guard stared at me really unnerved me.

His face flushed.

"Have you been crying?" he asked quietly.

I wiped my eyes and turned away from him. "That is none of your concern."

"Will you go back inside?" There was a softness to his voice now.

I looked up at the moon and the thousands of glittering stars that twinkled back down at me. I breathed in and out slowly, trying to calm myself down. "I will not escape, if that's what you mean."

When I turned around to face him, he had his hand on the sheath of a concealed dagger. I crossed my arms across my chest. "There is no danger up here. Besides, there is another guard posted outside my doorway," I paused. "I do not believe that I caught your name before."

He removed his hand from his dagger. "Wesley, my lady. Wesley Durant."

"Well, thank you, Wesley. I appreciate your efforts in obtaining my safety."

"Much obliged, my lady. I should probably get back to patrolling. The next shift will arrive soon, and it would not look good for either of us if I were found on your balcony, casually having a conversation with you."

"Oh, right. Goodnight then, Wesley."

He shimmied down the vines, picked up his staff, and disappeared beneath the moonlight. I went back into my room and slipped into bed.

CHAPTER
III

The next morning, my maids did not attend to me, as they promised they would last night. Instead, Queen Celine graced me with her presence, as I had just crawled out of bed. When she entered my room, I put my robe on and slid my feet into my silk slippers.

"So mother, do you actually have time for me today, or are you just checking up on me?" I greeted her bitterly.

She patted the space next to her on the bed. "Sit beside me. We have much to discuss."

I did as she said.

"My dear Adalia, it was never meant to be a permanent situation. After years of trying before finally carrying you and your late sister, there was an attempt made on my life by one of the attending nurses. After the two of you were born, we sent you off with Jacinta and Giles to be sure that at least one of the heirs was out of harm's way."

"I was the *spare*. Adelaide was the *heir*." I whispered between gritted teeth.

"The king's - that is, *your father's* - advisor, did not permit you to come home. Years flew by, but I visited in secret, and I regretted when I stopped coming to see you."

I turned to her. "I never knew that. Why?"

"Why, what?"

"Why did you stop coming to visit me?"

"My darling daughter, you were so innocent and did not know any different. It became too difficult to bear when you were about four years of age. You called the governess, *mother*. I felt as if I had lost you and then thought it would be better if you never knew. At least then, if someone came for you, you would know nothing about the monarchy. I did it to keep you safe and to protect the throne. Can you ever forgive me?"

"I think I can forgive you," I added, "In time." I paused for a moment to recollect my thoughts. "I would like to get to know you better."

Tears welled in the queen's eyes as she drew me in for a big bear hug. "I would like that very much."

By the time the afternoon rolled around, Queen Celine left my room to attend to her queenly duties. Whatever those were. I figured that, one day, I would find out what was actually required of me. For now, though, I was whisked away by Jacinta into an unused room on the fourth floor. Crisp, alabaster sheets covered the furniture. In the corner laid a mahogany grand piano. Jacinta moved out the piano's bench for her to sit while she instructed me in the art of table manners, speech etiquette, and walking.

By the end of the day, I was apparently still slouching. The dusty tomes fell from my head again.

"One more time, my flower." Jacinta instructed.

I sighed, picking up the books. "This is hopeless."

"Again." Jacinta gave me 'the look' she used to give me when I was defiant.

I placed the books atop my golden blonde

hair and began walking from one end of the room to the other side.

Jacinta opened up an old yellowed-page history book. She quizzed me as I walked. "When did Pembroke Palace become the official residence of the Royal Family?"

I kept my eyes focused on the back of the room. "After the raven, known as Queen Merlina, flew away from the Tower of London, the other ravens followed. Thus, leading people to believe in the age-old tale about the monarchy. It was believed that if the ravens, who guarded and watched over the Crown and the Tower of London, were to leave their residence, then the kingdom would fall. When they did all disappear, the monarchy decided it was time to move away from their home. That is why the Royal Family resides at Pembroke Palace now."

"What was the old palace called?"

"That is easy. Buckingham Palace."

"Why did the Whyndam family move to Pembroke rather than anywhere else in the United Kingdom?"

I sometimes answered this one incorrectly. I

stopped walking. The thick books wobbled for a moment. "Was it because of the legend?"

Jacinta nodded in approval. "Go on..."

"The original legend comes from Wales. So, the Royal Family wanted to honor the legend as well as create a new narrative for the monarchy. Matholwch, an Irish leader, mistreated the Princess Branwen. The King of the Britons, Branwen's brother, had Matholwch's head decapitated and buried to protect the kingdom from foreign invasion. The Whyndams spun the tale to their advantage, saying that White Hill was not where the Tower of London stood, as most had believed. They insisted that Matholwch's head was buried in Pembrokeshire in Wales. They inhabited Pembroke Castle and restored it, adding modern touches to the once medieval castle."

"Very good. You are forgetting about one thing. Margaret Beaufort gave birth to King Henry VII of England in this castle in the 1400s. The Whyndams took this castle as their home, mostly because of the legend, but also because royalty was born here as well. He was remembered as the first monarch of Tudor House. Your family still uses the Tudor rose as their national emblem to this day."

I began walking once more. "He is only remembered because he was the first of his dynasty."

Jacinta shook her head. "No, one of the greatest achievements and why he is still remembered to this day is because he united the royal Houses of York and Lancaster, thus ending the War of the Roses."

I stopped at the end of the room and removed the books from my head. I finally noticed the titles of the tomes in my hand: *The Royal Lines of Succession, Welsh Legends and Folktales,* and *The Language of Flowers*.

I raised an eyebrow. "Really? The Language of Flowers?"

Jacinta stood from the piano bench, "It is important to know the meanings of flowers in their different colors, especially when you will arrange bouquets for guests or even at your own wedding. Please read them and study the history of the lines of succession by the end of the week. We will resume our lessons in a few days. Until then…" She came and tapped a finger on the books before leaving me alone in the forgotten room.

A few hours had passed, and the sky turned a dark blood orange. The clouds passing by were tinged a rouge-like pink, almost salmon or coral colored. How I had wished I could paint the evening sky, instead of reading these time-worn books.

I sat on the ledge by the window and finally looked down. On the south side of the palace were about two dozen guards. All were training in hand-to-hand combat. Half of them wore loose white shirts. The other half were shirtless, with their chiseled torsos on full display.

I watched as one guard from each side battled it out. The shirtless guard parried and side-stepped the advances of his opponent. He had the other guard face-down on the ground in a matter of mere seconds.

When he turned around, I saw those familiar blue-green eyes staring back up at me. I moved away from the window. It was Wesley

Durant, and he definitely noticed me watching him. From my reflection in the window, I could tell that a blush swept into my cheeks. My face felt hot until I made it back to my room.

CHAPTER
IV

I was not sure that I could ever get used to being naked in front of strangers. I mean, all of my maids were very nice, but they were all essentially outsiders to me. Perhaps this was normal for Adelaide, but I was finding it harder to get used to.

Faith and Grace released me from my nightgown as Constance held out her hand to help me into the enormous bath. It was more like a jacuzzi than a bathtub, with jets and all.

Verity poured scented oils and even rose petals into the steaming water.

Eventually, my morning routine was becoming a habit to me. Undress. Bathe. Dress. Primp my hair and effortlessly put on makeup. Be escorted by my guard on duty to eat breakfast in the Great Hall. Eat breakfast. Attend lessons with Jacinta until lunch.

Occasionally, I saw Queen Celine whenever she could spare the time. I almost never saw King Cassian—except in passing. He was mainly in the East Wing of the palace.

I was still very limited by where I was allowed to go. I was almost never left alone. I cherished the evenings when I could have some "me time." Those were the hours when I was left in the room where I had my daily royal lessons or when I was left in my bedroom after dark.

I was disappointed when Wesley was not present outside the doorway to my room. One of the other guards, Officer Wyrmwood, greeted me instead and escorted me to the Great Hall.

I had grown accustomed to how my life at the palace would be from now on. I even started my days earlier, in the hopes of trying to attend at least one meal with the king and queen. It would have been nice if they had answered some of my questions about my role as princess.

As I arrived at the Great Hall. Per usual, the guards who opened the large double doors for me announced me.

"Princess Adelaide, arriving for breakfast," they declared in unison.

I entered and noticed that King Cassian and Queen Celine were already seated and being poured their morning beverages. The queen beamed, but King Cassian just looked back at his newspaper.

"Welcome, daughter," Queen Celine said. There was elegance in her voice, but it was also calming. In front of her husband, the king, she exhumed richness, while maintaining an air of kindness.

After Zachariah and the other white-gloved staff set our plates with our meal, King Cassian dismissed them. Even the guards closed the doors. I was surprised when the three of us were alone.

"I did not want them to overhear our conversation," mumbled the king.

"What are we to discuss today?" I asked. It had already been two weeks since I arrived and not once had we all sat down and had a meal together.

King Cassian looked me over and set down his article. "The staff tells me that my daughter is a changed girl, after the accident, but that every day you are returning to your old self."

Queen Celine smiled faintly. "That is encouraging to hear. Right, Adelaide?"

I twisted the poached eggs with my fork until the yolk leaked out, encompassing the bottom half of my scones. "Yes, I suppose that is encouraging. I have some questions that I would like to be answered truthfully. Since we are alone, that is."

The king and queen stopped eating and turned to me.

"When I first came here, I was told that a limited amount of people knew the truth about my sister and me. Who are these people?"

The queen brought her teacup to her mouth and sipped.

The king exhaled before answering, "Mr. and Mrs. Lockwood know, of course. My advisor, Sir Braham. Dr. Vennora, who delivered you and your sister. And finally, Nurse Jayne, but she and her doctor are no longer with us."

"What happened?"

"Dr. Vennora passed away six years ago. I had Sir Braham go to his medical facility and destroy the records he kept on all his patients. I had Nurse Jayne executed for trying to kill the queen while she was pregnant. Sir Braham retired some years ago. I personally sent him far away where he was rewarded for his service to me and to the Crown."

I continued to eat. "So, my maids and my guards do not know."

Queen Celine said, "No, but as your father said before, you are doing an excellent job pretending."

I decided to switch the subject. "Jacinta has me reading such … interesting books as of late. What about my learning will help me run the country?"

King Cassian stabbed an apple slice with his knife. "That will be many years from now. You will have your husband by your side then to guide you in matters of State."

Husband? "You cannot be serious? I am almost eighteen."

King Cassian chuckled. "Celine and I were already wed by then. That is how our world works. It is important for you to understand and study our past as a country and as a monarchy. You will not actually be running the entire show, though. That is for your husband to take over. After your marriage, you can hardly be expected to worry about the country. You will be far too busy managing your governess to take care of the next heirs, preferably males." The look he gave Queen Celine was heart-breaking. As if she could be blamed for having only daughters.

The queen stared daggers at him.

For the first time, I could see the facade of my parents' public image for the first time. I was excused for my ongoing lessons for the day.

CHAPTER
V

In the middle of my lessons with Jacinta, I stopped paying attention to anything she was saying. I could not get past what King Cassian said to me at breakfast. I didn't think that I could be the princess. I could barely stand the thought of the role now. How was I supposed to stand it when I was forced to marry? Most likely, I would not even be able to choose my own husband. I would have bet King Cassian or one of his advisors would set something up. I had never really thought about marrying someone. I had never even had a boyfriend, for crying out loud!

"What are you thinking about?" Jacinta asked. She looked saddened today and could sense when something was wrong, even before I realized it myself.

"All the duties, the studying, the walking on

eggshells … I don't know how much more of all this I can take," I confessed.

"You were born for this role, even if you were second. Being second only meant that your role was delayed."

"More like, I was second choice. You don't need to make me feel better."

"Oh. Believe me, I'm not trying to make you feel better. I am simply stating the facts."

"The facts are that this morning, they told me I would never rule the country. They told me that, basically, as soon as I come of age, I will be expected to find a husband."

Jacinta looked horrified. "I raised you to be kind, caring, and thoughtful of others. You possess all of those qualities and more. I have already spoken with many members of the staff. You know what each of them said?"

I shook my head.

"They told me that, at first, your moodiness was understandable, and that it was like nothing had changed. Then, as you became more familiar with Pembroke, and as you further accepted your role, they became proud of how you have changed for the better. They told me that you are finally turning into a princess who is worthy of their praise. It is only a matter of time before your people love you, as well."

"I appreciate the sentiments, but I can't be forced to marry someone I don't know."

"I will talk with the queen. Her lady's maid is a good friend of mine. Whatever transpired this morning, erase it from your memory. How are you doing with studying the royal lines of succession?"

"Fine. I actually enjoyed the *Language of the Flowers* more than I thought I would. I'd like to visit the gardens and list their meanings by name and color."

Jacinta smiled. "Perhaps after the Americans arrive. I do not believe that you are permitted to go outside until their visit commences."

"Will there be photographers?"

"I believe so. That is why your studies, and our lessons, are important. You only have two more weeks until your debut in society as Adelaide, officially."

That was what I was dreading most of all. I was afraid of what would happen if someone from Adelaide's past realized that there was something off with me. Then, the secret would be out. Would another assassin come for me? Why had they come before? It seemed odd that the country seemed so peaceful right now. Why would anyone want to destroy their beloved princess and the only heir? Did we have enemies in other countries?

Jacinta coughed suddenly, removing me from my destructive thoughts. She handed me a photo album. Inside there were pictures of me dancing at parties, cutting large ribbons at ceremonies, and posed at beautiful locations. I realized that these were pictures of my sister Adelaide at events. Some were from magazines and others were from newspaper articles. Next to each photograph was a handwritten caption.

"I thought that you might like to see what kinds of events you would be attending. Many of them look like fun. Imagine the gowns, the glitz, and the glamour of new places, and the handsome faces of some of these bachelors."

I laughed. "You know, you're not really helping the whole husband situation."

"That is another thing I would like to mention. There is one eligible prince that

Adelaide was photographed with at many events in recent years. I'd like you to learn some of the people's names in this album. When the Americans arrive, they will have also met most of these people. The president's son was also someone whom Adelaide met before. Luckily, we have good ties with the Americans, and he has not visited in maybe three or four years. You can always use the excuse of recovering from your ordeal, or you may say that many things have changed since you two last saw one another. Either way, you are to make him and his parents feel welcomed."

"I understand. Are there any notes about some of these people besides their name and country?"

"Yes, there are footnotes in the back of the album."

CHAPTER
VI

The next week rolled by as if it were a movie playing in slow motion. I accomplished the same monotonous tasks. My studies were improving. According to Jacinta, I was quite the protégé in all things royal, considering the little time we had spent to prepare me.

The Americans were coming in another week, and I was not sure how I felt about it. I knew that I could probably pass as my sister, Adelaide, now with knowing almost everything she must've been learning. I was growing more and more aware of the fact that, after the Americans' State Dinner, there was no going back. Thus far, the public had not seen Adelaide and for all the people knew, she could actually have been dead. If it weren't for me taking her place and pretending to become her, that is. I was sure that her assassin would be reeling with the news once they saw me. Perhaps that's what King Cassian and Queen Celine wanted: to make their enemies think that we were untouchable. If only they knew the truth.

With everything going on, the staff was preparing for the Americans' arrival. I learned that for every staff member I ran into, there must be at least five to ten more behind them. From time to time, I would hear the clatter of footsteps from behind the walls of the hallways. I knew that there must be a network of servant's corridors adjacent to the halls of the palace. They were constantly moving around now. Decorations were being put up. I enjoyed the blue dyed roses. From my readings of the *Language of the Flowers*, blue roses meant attaining the impossible.

While the Royal Family's emblem remained the red and white Tudor Rose, the Americans national flower was the mysterious blue rose. Of course, no such rose could be found in nature, but the white roses stained with a deep royal blue were definitely a sight to see.

It was such a warm, muggy day for early

October. With all the humidity, I was not dressed very royal today. My maids had braided plaits into my hair and tied the ends with lime green ribbons. They really stood out in my golden blonde hair. The pastel green fitted tank top and khaki pants reminded me of my time in the country. Even King Cassian and Queen Celine wore loose fitting clothing as well. They still had all the windows shut, and the entrances blocked off. Adelaide was still supposed to be recovering, and they did not want any photographers within the walls yet.

My relationship with my parents had become less strained since the beginning of my time here. I was learning more and more about them and the kind of people they actually were, beneath their pompous royal images. They did well at masking themselves. I didn't even mind when I heard the occasional yelling fits and disagreements they had. It just proved to me that marriage was hard work, and it made them seem more normal to me. Everything was not always perfect, nor should it be.

I was halfway through my dill-pickle-and-sauerkraut soup when we heard a loud crash from outside the edge of the Great Hall.

The two guards outside the hall stomped their staffs and barely got out the names of their announcement before three people dressed exquisitely pushed open the doors to the Great Hall themselves.

"The American President Oliver Smith ... his beautiful wife, the First Lady Irene Smith ... and the First Son Aiden Smith," the guards announced, faster than usual, trying to say their names before the strangers could walk in.

The president and his son were dressed in sharp, cadet blue suits. Aiden was the spitting image of his father, with his sandy cropped hair and striking wintergreen eyes. The only difference was that Oliver Smith had silver streaks scattered throughout his hair, and some wrinkles on his forehead and around his eyes.

I had not expected the twinkle in Aiden's eyes as he gave me a little wink and a devilish smirk before stopping at our table.

After taking us all in, the first lady said, "Oh, dear. It looks as if we have ruined an intimate family gathering."

President Smith stepped forward in front of

his family. "Your Royal Highness, Princess Adelaide, we are so glad that you are feeling better from your vicious attack."

Everyone dropped their forks. The queen rang her little silver bell for the staff to clear our plates. "If you'll excuse us, then we will welcome you properly in the Receiving Room." She made eye contact with me. "Adelaide, please have your maids dress you for the occasion."

Aiden moved to the left side of the table and extended his arm to me. "It has been some time since we have seen each other, Your Highness. Allow me to escort you. That way, we can catch up," he offered.

I had no idea what to say.

The queen interrupted us. "She would be delighted." She added, "I'll send for Constance to meet you in your room, Adelaide. Do show the first son the mirrored hallway on your way up."

I knew she meant to say to take the long way to my room. I scooched my chair back, dabbing my napkin in the corner of my lips, leaving the napkin folded on my plate. I took Aiden's arm and did not look back as we exited into the hallway.

Our conversation was casual at first. Then, he started making me feel uncomfortable.

"It killed me to read that news article about you." Aiden said.

"Oh? I was unaware of it." What in the world was he talking about?

"I was very sad to hear about your ordeal a month ago."

"Let's change the subject. I really do not wish to relive what happened." Also, because I had *no idea* what happened. I knew about as much as everyone else. King Cassian and Queen Celine never exactly told me the details … other than Adelaide did not survive her assassination. To the public, Adelaide lived on, with nothing but head trauma and a foggy memory.

I led him round the corner towards the mirrored hallway. It was breathtaking, with all the mirrors and stained glass. It was strange to see our reflection in the mirrors. I was very out of place with my braided plaits, but standing next to Aiden, I could not deny that we looked good together.

"How is your memory? I had heard things upon my arrival."

I whipped my head at him. "Who told you that?"

"Ah, if I revealed my source then they would get into trouble." He teased.

I shrugged, trying to show indifference. "My memory is getting better every day."

He paused, and I realized that we were alone. There were no crimson uniforms nearby. Nobody was patrolling this hallway. I was unsure whether it was on purpose or not.

"Do you remember the last time we saw one another, Adelaide?"

It was a good thing that I memorized all the footnotes from Jacinta's photo album. "Christmas, three years ago?"

He squinted his eyes at me and furrowed his eyebrow.

Had I misspoken? Wasn't that correct? I knew it was. But why do I get the feeling as if something is off?

I sighed in relief as Aiden continued walking. "We really should be going towards my room. I have been stationed in the West Wing recently."

"Yes, I thought it strange that my family and I were being put up in the East Wing of Pembroke. I do not believe that I have ever had the pleasure of being on that side of the palace before. I am aware that the king and queen's suites are there."

I nodded. My heart about stopped as soon as I finally saw the crimson uniform of a guard outside my room at the end of the hall. I halted for a moment.

Aiden looked beyond my stare and focused on the guard outside my room. "I think you can handle walking the rest of the way yourself." Aiden stopped us and turned me around, so that my back was facing Officer Durant.

Aiden grabbed the ends of one of my braids and stared down at me with those emerald eyes. He bit his lip, contemplating something he wanted to ask me. "So, you do not remember Christmas after all?"

"I am not sure I know what you mean?" My response sounded more like a question than an actual statement.

Aiden leaned in closer to me, inches from my face. "I asked you for a kiss beneath the mistletoe."

I moved back a step and tapped my head, uncomfortably laughing. "Foggy memory, remember?"

"You rejected me, kind of like this. Stepping away from my advances. You told me that if you wanted an acceptance for that request, then I would have to prove myself to you. That I was indeed worthy to kiss a princess."

I did not know what to do. I could feel my face burning. I had never been kissed, and this was not how I wanted my first kiss to be ... especially not in the company of my guard— and not just any guard. Wesley Durant had become a constant in my ever-changing life as a royal.

I was so nervous; I practically cried out my answer, "You'll just have to prove yourself if you want a kiss from me!" I did not wait to see his response. I spun on my heel and practically ran down the hall.

As I approached my room, Wesley turned and opened the door for me, saying, "Shall I prove myself to you as well?"

We locked eyes before I passed him by and

walked through the doorway. Constance was waiting for me. She helped me into an evening gown; a navy fitted mermaid style dress with little rhinestones that glittered as I moved. The low neckline met with sheer sleeves that ran down my arms, bedazzled with jewels. I knew that I would not be able to raise my arms very high. I was hoping that I would not need to. I was only supposed to make small talk and smile. That was my duty as a welcoming hostess.

By the time I was done sliding into the gown, Verity and Grace entered.

"Wow, Your Highness. That dress looks like the night sky. It is very beautiful," Grace complimented me.

"Thank you." That was one of the first times that she ever said anything to me.

Untrue to her name, Grace accidentally hit her hip on my vanity table, knocking over one of the perfume bottles.

Constance hissed at her like a cat. "Clean that up this instant."

"It's fine. Really, Grace," I said. "You can deal with it later when I leave."

I was starting to realize that each of my maids seemed to be the opposite of their namesakes. Grace was not graceful or eloquent at all. In fact, she was more of a klutz than I was—and *that* was saying something. Faith was definitely a talker, but everything that came out of her mouth was dripping with pessimism. She did not have faith in herself or in other people, it seemed. She might've made a better lawyer than a maid. At least, her pessimistic ways were enough to play devil's advocate in a courtroom argument. Constance was not very constant. She was never on time when she was summoned, and her moods changed with the wind. Verity had not spoken a word to me in the three weeks I had known her. She was very efficient. I wish I had studied the meanings of names, instead of flowers, in my books from Jacinta. I desperately wished to know what the meaning of Verity was. Perhaps her name meant "the chatty one." It would have made the most sense if she were opposite, like the others. Perhaps she was mute?

Instead of asking her, I kept quiet as Verity took out my braids and wrapped my wavy locks into a low side bun. On the other side of my head, Grace entwined midnight blue jewels into my hair. They stood out amongst my golden strands.

When Constance pulled out a large velvet box and unclasped the lid, a gasp escaped me. Before me was a deep set of sapphires braided into a crisscrossing design with a diamond the size of my big toe dangling in the middle. I refused immediately. I personally did not feel worthy of wearing such an elaborate piece.

"In the past, you would never turn down such a statement piece." Constance said.

"The necklace suits you, Your Highness," Grace said quietly.

"I appreciate all that you have done, but I am only greeting our guests. Perhaps I can wear something like that at a more formal occasion."

"Of course. We just thought that you would like to impress the Presidential Son, that's all."

"Why would I want to do that?"

"Because we remember your bargain from that one Christmas. Besides, we know he likes you. He was always trying to snag your attention, but you never gave him the time of day since he was not even a royal and therefore…" Grace stopped herself.

All three of us stared at her.

"Out with it!" I declared.

Grace's face turned rouge. Even in speech, she was not true to her name. "Um, it is not appropriate for me. Forgive me, I spoke out of turn."

I rolled my eyes at her. "Please … nothing you say in here will ever get you into trouble. At least, not with me."

She nodded. "Thank you, Your Highness. You once said that since he was not a royal, he was therefore not worth your time. I figured that was why you were caught in the Prince of Monaco's arms, instead of kissing Aiden Smith beneath the mistletoe that year."

Such a confession shocked me. "I am afraid that I do not remember saying that. Thank you for your honesty. Perhaps Aiden Smith will surprise me tonight."

My three maids curtsied.

I looked in the mirror, and scarcely recognized myself with all the makeup. This was the first time I think I truly looked like

Adelaide. Even though we shared the same face, makeup was not the facade for her. Adelaide must've played the part of the princess and she have been expected to be the embodiment of etiquette and finesse. Now that role and duty fell to me. With one last look at myself, I now knew that all the glitter and jewels were to be my sword and shield in all of this. I would wield them fiercely to my advantage.

CHAPTER VII

Wesley Durant was utterly speechless. He cleared his throat as he did a once over of me. Twice. He extended his arm, which I gladly took. "You look like the night sky."

"Thank you." I stumbled forward, tripping on my strappy high heels, but he caught me with his other arm. As he steadied me, I told him what was on my mind. "What you said earlier when I came back to my room after meeting with the Presidential Son, was out of line. You have no need to prove yourself to me. You are my guard and can be nothing more."

Wesley's face darkened as he beheld me. "I understand. Forgive me, princess."

He moved to my side. There was distance between us, and it wasn't physical.

I continued to hold his arm as he escorted me to the Receiving Room in the East Wing of the palace.

Breaking the silence, I said, "I want you to know that I trust you with my life, as you are my royal guard, and with the details of my safety only."

Before leaving me at the entrance, he whispered, "I had always wondered how long it would take for you to regain your memory. Congratulations, princess. You have turned back into the royal you were before."

Wesley turned to leave before I could say anything. I hated that he used words like *princess* and *a royal* like it was bad. From his mouth, he made them sound like curses.

There was only one guard stationed outside the door that announced my name. I was left feeling disappointed that Wesley walked away from me before I could say anything more, but I forced myself to wear a smile as the doors opened for me.

The Receiving Room was a floral mess. The wallpaper, from floor to ceiling, was the absolute worst. Tiny cream-colored baby's breath and pastel pink peonies, set on a tan background, reminded me of a different time.

The beige lounge chairs and loveseats were just as bad. It looked like the room of an old cat-lady from another era.

Aiden slicked back the longer strands of his sandy blonde hair to the side. He still wore his crisp blue-grey suit. It did nothing for his wintergreen eyes. I let myself wonder what Wesley would look like in that blue-grey suit, instead of his crimson and black uniform. His eyes would sparkle like aquamarines. I shook my head. I would not let Wesley disturb my thoughts this evening. I was meant to be interested in all things American.

Aiden offered me a crystal glass of burgundy port. I took the glass and greeted Oliver and Irene Smith. His parents bowed and curtsied to me respectively, then turned their attentions back to the king and queen. The four of them were having a serious conversation.

"Do you play chess?" I asked Aiden.

"A little. I do not have much time for games recently."

We moved over to the chessboard on the glass table by the roaring fireplace. I sat on the beige loveseat. Aiden took his place across from me in the leather armchair. It was the only piece of furniture that was masculine in this entire room.

"Tell me, what is new with you? I have not seen you in the last three years."

He looked bored with his empty wine glass. "Nothing much is new on my end. Last time, I was finishing my secondary education and was preparing for Harvard. Of course, I was accepted. I decided to take a gap year, though. I traveled by yacht and sailed the Panama Canal and traveled around the Caribbean a bit this past year."

"That sounds amazing." I tried acting happy for him, masking my jealousy inside. I wanted to explore the world for myself. I had only ever seen the twelve acres of land of the country estate gated in by the wrought-iron fence.

"I would love to sail the South of France on the Mediterranean, though. I hear those waters are serene. I was envious of those photos of you last summer."

I blanched. Absolutely blanched. I did not remember any photos of me on a yacht in the photo album Jacinta gave me. I was completely frozen.

Aiden must have sensed my discomfort. He continued, "I believe you were there with friends." He paused mid-sentence while removing one of my pawns from the chessboard. "Visiting that French prince, no doubt."

"Perhaps I will order the American tabloids and newspapers from the last three years surrounding you and your family."

"All of those are rubbish. Nothing is to be believed."

"Precisely. Being in the public eye yourself, you must be aware that most things that are written about us are most likely false."

He stopped his boorish expression and stared at me directly, while Zachariah came by and offered to pour Aiden another glass of wine. When Zachariah was done, he moved to the other side of the Receiving Room, handing out the bottle for refreshments.

Aiden smirked. I feared his tongue was going to be forked at the end. "So, the rumors are not true then?"

I forced out a laugh. "I must say that I do not

read the papers about myself. I prefer not to. Clearly, you have been busy reading them about me. Tell me, Aiden, what do you believe to be true?"

We were interrupted by King Cassian's booming chuckles as he embraced the president. Oliver Smith pulled back and shook the king's hand vigorously, like they'd just made the pact of the century.

Aiden gulped down half his glass of wine. "That is never a good sign. It seems that they have concocted a scheme together." Aiden moved his black knight in front of my white king. "Checkmate."

I scanned the remaining pieces on the board. There was nothing that could be done except to sacrifice my queen. If I took his knight with my queen, then his black rook was positioned to strike her. I had no choice, so I did.

Aiden's eyes danced in the light of the fireplace. "You are learning. Good."

"Sorry?" I questioned.

"The queen is good to go wherever she wants … but then she knows her duty is to come back to the king," he said wickedly.

I got the sense that we were not talking about the game of chess anymore. Was he talking about Adelaide's prince, the one whom Grace had spoken of earlier? Was I supposed to pretend to be in love with the Prince of Monaco? Was Adelaide herself in love with this person? Why did he irk Aiden so much, besides being the boy whom Adelaide accepted a kiss from? There was clearly more history that I knew nothing of ... things that would not be found in Jacinta's footnotes. Tomorrow, I would seek out Grace and demand that she tells me everything. She always had her gossiping ear to the ground.

It was clear that Aiden was going to win the game of chess. I stood and made my excuses. Aiden left the chessboard and walked near me as we went to join our parents.

Queen Celine looked horrified. Her face was ghostly pale from something that Lady Irene said.

The first lady was a willowy woman. She was tall, and her beauty was ethereal. Her brown hair was swept to the side in cascading waves. Her peridot jewelry accented her eyes and garden-green gown.

When she spoke, though, her voice was commanding and not lovely at all. "I am looking forward to the State Dinner. It will be your first time with the paparazzi again, is it not?"

I nodded.

"Have your head maid send a fabric swatch over to my room. I wish for our families to be in coordinating colors for the event." She said before excusing herself to retire for the evening.

Aiden had moved to be with his mother as she exited the room.

I turned toward Queen Celine. "What was that about? Is it appropriate for them to dress the same at such a public event?"

Queen Celine patted my shoulder gently. "Do not concern yourself with that. At least for now. The State Dinner is still scheduled for two weeks from now. They were not supposed to arrive this early, and I was not in the mood to change the invitations. Many things can happen between now and then." Queen Celine removed her satin glove and took a petite appetizer from the silver tray held by Zachariah.

As he left us, she said, "How was your evening with the boy? Are you two getting along?"

"If you are asking if he suspects anything different with me, then I think it went well."

"Very well. Off you go then. You will have a big day tomorrow, now that they have arrived. Their unprecedented timing complicates matters."

Aiden came up from behind us. "Adelaide, would you accompany us on the hunt tomorrow morning?"

"No, I do not believe I will. Thank you for asking."

Queen Celine gave me that look. The look told me I had done something wrong.

I sucked in some air and breathed it out slowly. "What I mean to say is that I am still recovering, and I am not saddling my mare anytime soon. However, I would be delighted to go for a paddleboat ride in the pond by the gardens."

Queen Celine chimed in. "There will be a guard stationed with you both. I will see to it that both of you are under adequate supervision."

Aiden bowed to the queen, then took my hand in his and placed a chaste kiss on the back of it. "Sweet dreams, Adelaide. I shall retrieve you after the hunt."

I found the queen on my way out the door again. "Goodnight," I said.

"Tomorrow you will be a generous hostess. There will be photographers at the palace wanting to catch a glimpse of you since your recovery. Your father needs positive press these days. Make us proud."

CHAPTER VIII

I did not sleep well last night at all. My dreams were plagued with nightmares. Faith and Grace covered my dark circles with a thick coat of powders and creams. They insisted that if I fell into the pond that my makeup would stay intact. Verity let it slip that her name means "truth" and also that that boy, Aiden, is divine and if I don't want him, then she will take him for herself. I was contemplating if that was a truth or a lie.

They were giggling and told me it's as if I didn't remember how to flirt like I had once before. Apparently, Adelaide had had many suitors. I had to remind myself not to get tripped up with all the lies. I told them that I did not remember, and they said my memories will come back all in good time.

I was thrown into a simpler gown than the

one I wore last night. The sunset-peach dress had a sweetheart neckline and little capped sleeves. It was tied at the waist with a pink glittery bow that matched the ribbon on my straw sun hat. I wriggled my fingers into light pink, lace gloves to complete my sunny outfit.

I was met by Aiden's knock on the door. He had a picnic basket ready in his hand and a bottle of wine in the other. He bowed upon seeing me.

"You may stand up now, Aiden." I said and put a hand to my mouth to hide my smile like a proper lady should. No. Like the regal princess I am.

The click of a camera shutter snagged my attention. I took Aiden's arm and was keenly aware of his nature to impress me while the cameras were rolling. I knew that the royal photographers were going to be skulking about the palace. What I did not know was that they were trailing us. They could practically hear our every word in conversation. I leaned into Aiden to whisper so that those who were behind us could not hear. "It seems that my mother was true to her word about our adequate supervision."

Aiden chuckled. "Yes. You once used to revel in the attention. Do I sense a change of heart?"

I nodded slightly. "I have not completely recovered from my ordeal. I have headaches every now again and my memories are slowly coming back to me. I do not want these photographers to sense any weakness on my part."

"I can respect that, Your Highness. I, too, am viewed harshly by the public because of who my father is. I find my role a bit hard to play at times, but then I remember that without my role, I would not be out in the sunshine with your beautiful self."

I rolled my eyes. "You, sir, are too kind."

We walked around the garden maze. More photographers were hiding about the bushes. I made a mental note to tell the queen that her idea of a dozen photographers was *not* my idea of "a few people from the press snapping a few photos." This was an invasion of privacy.

Aiden and I kept our conversation light and short while strolling about. He plucked a pink dahlia from the garden and knelt before me.

"For you, Princess Adelaide."

I hesitated. Why the dahlia flower? Out of all the flowers in this garden. Could Aiden have known? No, I decided. He just called me by her name. I accepted the dahlia and went to take it from his grasp, but he stood before me and strewn it into my hair behind my ear. It was a swift and bold gesture. I could not help but notice that the cameras clicked several times when Aiden was kneeling, holding out the flower and now as his hand lingered on my cheek from placing my flower behind my ear. I could see the magazine title: *Chivalry was not dead in the modern era.*

The only thing that unsettled me was the sinking feeling that somehow this was all a charade. I looked past Aiden, noticing how close we were, and moved away. Aiden turned around to see whom I was staring at.

"Officer Durant. What a pleasure it is to see you."

Wesley bowed before us. "I am to escort you both on your paddle boat ride."

"Very well then." I said, trying not to make eye contact. Of all the guards available in the palace, why did it have to be him?

Aiden greeted Officer Durant and shoved the picnic basket and bottle of wine in his arms. "If you do not mind, Officer, I'd be grateful if you could lighten my load so that I may escort the princess myself."

Wesley took the basket and bottle and gritted his teeth.

Aiden came next to me and put a hand to the small of my back, ushering me toward the pond. He helped me into the boat while Wesley laid out the blanket and opened the basket, emptying our picnic out on the shoreline.

I went to the front of the boat and took two oars in each hand.

Wesley turned and went to help but was stopped by Aiden. "I am perfectly capable of protecting the princess while we are on the boat. Perhaps you can stand by and watch from the shoreline for anyone that might disturb us, if you know what I mean. I hear that nearby the willow over there is good for some shade from this heat and for, uh, privacy."

I could hardly argue with the president's son, and I *did* want a little privacy from the photographers. The feeling of constantly being watched, and photos being taken, was unnerving to me. However, I did not approve of why Aiden was suggesting the need for privacy.

Wesley nodded. "Do not be out of sight for too long. Else I will come after you to ensure her safety."

Aiden was satisfied with that and hopped into the boat. There was barely enough room for the two of us. I allowed Aiden to take the oars as I sat at the front. The wind picked up and tore off my hat. "Oh! My hat!"

Aiden smiled more genuinely than he had when we were in the gardens earlier. "Whatever will you do without your hat?"

"Are you making fun of me?"

"Of course not, Your Highness. I would not dare. Although, I do recall your fondness for fashion. Perhaps not everything about you has changed."

"Or maybe my memory is coming back in strides."

"Does my princess bid me to retrieve her hat for her?" Aiden asked. His long lashes flickered.

I looked around for my hat, which floated away from us. It was nearly at the other end of the pond. I realized we were drifting in the direction of the weeping willow tree.

"Aiden, turn around. The branches are too thick. It will overturn the boat."

"Nonsense." He said as he kept rowing.

I could not swim, and Adelaide knew how. This was how the world would know that I was not her ... because I would drown. I was literally going to drown in my fears.

"It will be a nice area for us." Aiden said as he rowed faster.

I tried to stand up but wobbled unsteadily in the boat. "I thought that you wanted to go in the shade of the willow tree, not beneath it. Aiden, there are only rocks over there." I could not tell him that I could not swim if the boat flipped. I leaned forward, inching my way towards him, which he mistook my reasonings and shifting closer to me as well, dropping the oars. His weight was too much as he tried to meet me in the middle of this cramped paddle boat.

"Aiden!" I screamed as the boat hit the rocks

and flipped us over. The water was piercingly cold. It was such a shock to my body that I froze as I sank down, deeper and deeper into the pond, until I touched the thick mud at the bottom. I did not even try to swim. I knew that I could not, and I did not want those pesky photographers to capture my failure. I exhaled what little breath was left in my chest. The bubbles escaped my nose and floated upwards. I reached my hand toward the dim light of the surface. An overwhelming sense of dread coursed through me as my lungs tightened.

Then, I felt something skim my fingertips. I felt a strong, calloused hand grasp mine, and I was being lifted through the murkiness of the pond.

As my head breached the surface, I coughed up water violently. Someone's muscular arm was around my waist. My vision was blurry as water dripped down my face from my drenched hair. The next moment, I was being pulled onto shore. I vomited up more water and bits of my breakfast into the mud. Someone held my hair as I wretched.

When I had finished, I rolled onto my back. I

blinked until I saw the person hunched over me. Blue-green eyes looked at me, concerned.

"Wesley?"

"You frightened me, my lady. Are you well enough to stand?" He asked.

I tried to sit up as pain rang through my head. I had a blindingly painful headache. I squinched my eyes shut. I felt Wesley's arms go behind my back and beneath my knees. He picked me up effortlessly and cradle carried me until we were in the palace's infirmary.

I did not know where Aiden went and did not care at this point because here in Wesley's arms, I felt right at home.

I vaguely remembered when Wesley laid me gently down onto the infirmary's cot and when my maids helped me out of my wet dress into one of my nightgowns. By the time my aching head hit the pillow, I was drifting off to sleep.

~

When I woke up, nobody was around. From the darkness of the window, I reckoned it was already night. It was eerie being alone in the infirmary. My head still ached, but it was not as bad as it was before. I peeled back the sheet and put my bare feet on the cold floor. My maids had not left me a robe to cover up.

I left the infirmary and walked around aimlessly. Where was everyone? This must have been the East Wing of the palace. I was not yet familiar with this wing. I ran behind a suit of armor in the unfamiliar hallway as I heard two male voices whispering angrily. Two figures stopped short in front of the suit. I inched back farther, until I felt the wall behind me. By the light of candelabra, I saw that the voices belonged to Aiden and his father.

"Your job was simple. How could you mess up a boat ride? The paparazzi got pictures instead of that overprotective guard claiming to be the hero. I thought that she could swim…"

Aiden interrupted his father. "Must be her head injury. She is different from how she was before."

"At least, she pays more attention to you now. The last time I tried to forge an alliance, the king refused, based on her indifference towards you. This time, though, he will reconsider,"

Oliver Smith hissed.

"I know that this is important to you, father. I will not let you down."

I stayed behind the suit of armor, until I could no longer hear their voices. Then I ran back to the infirmary as fast as I could.

What were the Americans planning? What did the king have to reconsider?

CHAPTER IX

I had spent the next three days in the infirmary. The royal physician came by to check on me and told everyone else that it was not serious. My maids told me that there was a great commotion upstairs and that all the staff members behind the scenes were fussing over decorations for the State Dinner. It was to be a joyous occasion, I was told.

Aiden came to visit me and to apologize for not listening to me on the boat. He brought me a bouquet of dahlias from the garden. They cheered up the scenery of crisp white hospital beds and brought some color into the room. I was too chicken to ask him about what I had overheard the other night. I kept telling myself that perhaps I'd heard things wrong or had taken the meaning out of context.

The person I needed to see was my father, the

king. Even though I was the princess, I still had difficulty arranging a meeting to speak with him.

The only person that I had not seen was Wesley Durant. I wanted to thank him for saving me and for not telling anyone else that I could not swim. People may have suspected, but since the royal physician mentioned that my blindingly painful headache could be the reason I clammed up and did not swim to the surface myself; it would have to satisfy the disbelievers.

As I made my way back to the West Wing of the palace, I noticed all the decorations. It was strange that our royal emblem of the Tudor Rose was wrapped in the American blue rose petals. The roses were intertwined and created a new red, white, and blue design. Two olive branches looked as if they were sprouting from the roses' stems. I knew that the olive branch was meant to represent President Oliver Smith and his namesake. Even the first lady's name, Irene, meant *peace*. I'd have to reference the book of name meanings again to figure out Aiden's. It was one that I did not remember reading up on; perhaps I had never cared before.

There was a new guard outside my room, I noticed as I walked by him. He had a small X tattoo on his neck, beneath his hairline, under his ear.

"Your Highness, I was instructed that you should wear something extravagant today for the announcement and the State Dinner," Constance said as she unzipped a large hanging bag. Billowing, royal blue skirts spilled from the bag. The shade of blue was so vivid. The corset bodice had an elegant, draped pattern. Sheer, flesh-colored fabric wrapped along the sweetheart neckline and went down the sleeves. The fabric transitioned from a modest design to an intricate jeweled pattern from the forearm to the wrist.

I stared at my reflection in the mirror as Faith was weaving little dyed blue roses into my golden blonde locks. Grace fastened a deep blue cape that attached to the back of my dress and flowed like it was a long train behind me. Verity, who barely talked, was humming to herself harmoniously.

"Verity, what has you in a good mood all of a

sudden?" I asked her.

Verity giggled but stopped as Constance eyed her like a hawk.

"I think that everyone is simply excited about all the festivities today. The State Dinner is very important. It shows that our two countries are at peace, and it displays the unity of our alliance with one another," Grace said as she moved to my side.

Verity looked like she might explode. "Oh, can't we just tell her!"

Faith and Grace had a deer-in-the-headlights look about them. Their eyes widened.

With the flick of her wrist, Constance dismissed Verity.

She winked, saying, "Good luck," before leaving us.

Constance placed the silver-and-diamond tiara that the queen had given me on my head to complete the look.

Constance opened the doors as Grace and Faith picked up my skirts and cape behind me, making sure that their masterpiece did not get ruined.

The guard to my left just kept staring forward.

Maybe nobody had told him about his escorting duties. No matter. I decided that my maids were company enough for me. Constance lingered in the doorway as if she was going to say something to the new guard on duty but closed her mouth instead.

A flash of aquamarine caught my attention. "Officer Durant," I said as he stopped, almost passing me by.

"My lady." He barely acknowledged me.

I dismissed my maids. "Wesley, I wanted to thank you for saving my life."

He said nothing. He played with one of his buttons on his uniform.

"In secret, I never actually learned how to swim."

His expression changed. Confusion flickered. "My lady, last summer you dove off of a boat and floated in the very same pond, much to your parents' dismay."

Oh, no. I've done it again. How do I backpedal from this?

"Well, since my incident ... um, since then, I do not remember how to swim."

"My lady, do I need to fetch the physician for

you? You are struggling with your words here."

I contemplated telling him the truth right then and there.

"Princess Adelaide, you are most radiant." Aiden announced as he approached us. He was dressed in a cream suit lined with gold thread. A single crimson red rose wavered on his lapel. It seemed as I was dressed like the American blue rose, Aiden's suit was fashioned in the Tudor Rose colors. On his cuffs was the design of a golden lion, the symbol of England. His sandy hair was slicked back. He looked good. He looked like a prince. He waved a hand in front of Wesley. "You may go. You are not needed here any longer."

Wesley turned on his heel and continued down the hall.

"How *dare* you? Aiden, you may dismiss your own Secret Service members, but you may not be so callous with my guard."

He raised his brow, questioning, "*Your* guard, Your Highness?"

Heat rose to my face. I was mad now. "Anyone of my guards, maids, or palace staff. You are a guest here; in case you have forgotten. This is my home. Not yours."

Aiden grins while saying, "There's the old Adelaide I remember. Seems like yesterday's dip in the cold water must've shocked your system."

"Not quite." I looked behind me, but Wesley was already gone.

I took Aiden's arm, and we walked into the Grand Hall together. He was situated next to me today, and we were farther away from the Smiths and the king and queen. We ate breakfast cordially and mainly in silence.

When I noticed Aiden studying me, it made me uncomfortable. "Why do I feel as though I am the only one who does not seem to know what is happening today?"

Aiden finished swallowing his piece of bacon before answering me. "Adelaide, the State Dinner is indeed important," he said bluntly.

The king and queen were more positive and loving today—although I had no idea why. Even the president and first lady's spirits seemed to have risen, as well.

I whispered back to him, "Seriously, though, what is going on? Why is everyone so cheerful this morning?"

"Our fathers are making some sort of announcement today. Something about our two countries coming together as allies." Aiden grabbed another scone. "You know, all that nonsense of peace and harmony. Blah, blah, blah, blah, blah."

I patted my napkin at the corners of my mouth. "Wow, I do not believe you have ever been that abrupt with me."

"I have a feeling that you will have to get used to it."

I so badly wanted to say, *only until you leave tomorrow, after the State Dinner is over.* Common sense won, so I kept my mouth shut.

As the staff took away our breakfast, everyone moved towards the balcony. Down below were thousands of civilians. I instinctively grasped Aiden's hand.

He whispered in my ear, "Since when are you afraid of the spotlight?"

"I was not expecting all these people so soon after my recovery. The king and queen promised that your family would be the first big audience before I resumed my duties."

King Cassian and Queen Celine moved gracefully toward the main dais. The Americans halted behind them, to their left.

"Good people of England," King Cassian said powerfully. "Today is a momentous day, not only for our country but also for our royal family. A very long time ago, the United States of America were once a part of our great empire. We are no longer the same British Empire as we once were, but my ancestors before me unified our many kingdoms. That is why we are known as the United Kingdom of Great Britain and Northern Ireland. Our kingdoms are made up of England, Scotland, Wales, and Northern Ireland."

King Cassian looked behind him at the Americans. "Today we add another to our illustrious name."

The crowd hushed. It was so silent that we could only hear the wind whistling.

I looked up at Aiden, who shrugged. Whatever the king was about to say would be news to him, as well.

The king went on with his grand speech. "President Oliver Smith of the United States of

America has agreed to step down. He will be the last American president."

Whispers of shock, concern, and confusion rippled through the crowd.

Aiden stepped forward, but then moved back next to me. He was holding in whatever he wanted to say. I looked down below us and noticed the cameramen and press hanging on my father's every word. No doubt that this speech would be analyzed later.

"The United States of America will once again merge and become one with our great United Kingdom. Our lands have always been united and today they will become one in an even more permanent way."

President Smith stepped forward, adding, "Thank you, King Cassian, for your generous hospitality. Lady Irene and I cannot thank you enough. To all of our peoples, together we will be the greatest powerhouse nation that the world has ever known. Any threats made against us on either continent will be dealt with. I was horrified to learn about our dear Princess Adelaide's assassination attempt. She is beloved by all and especially has become a dear part of our Smith family."

Aiden and I both looked at each other with that statement. What did President Smith mean when he said I was a dear part of the American family? We watched on as President Smith finished his piece.

"…with that being said, I will be the last American president, and more details will emerge at a later point in time. Today, our children will sign a peace treaty with the terms of our new, true alliance." President Smith paused dramatically, as Lady Irene and Queen Celine stood beside their husbands. "Our two households will also merge, along with our two great nations. My son, Aiden Valentine Smith, will be wed to Princess Adelaide Rosalind Isadora Elita Whyndam."

A roaring cheer and a thunderous applause erupted from the crowd.

I think I may have stopped breathing. It was like I was underwater again. Drowning and frozen. Unable to move until I hit rock bottom. Out of the corner of my eye, Aiden gulped. With a crooked grin, his hands wrapped around my waist. He pulled me closer to him and he brought his lips down to meet mine in a tender kiss. This was my first kiss, and it was done in front of hundreds of thousands of people. I tried toning out the deafening applause. Aiden was playing with the crowd as he dipped me, prolonging our kiss.

As he lifted me back up, he moved his lips against my neck. "Smile," he said, barely above a whisper.

I almost hadn't heard him say it amongst the cheers and well-wishes. I did as he commanded. I smiled from ear to ear. I was in shock.

So, this was what it truly means to be a princess … to have no control over my own life, to be a pawn on the king's chessboard. This was what it meant to step into my sister's shoes at last.

CHAPTER
X

I had never had an out-of-body experience before, but I believed that this moment in time was one. It was like I was watching myself in slow motion. I was moving, and doing things, but not able to speak up or stop myself. This was like a bad movie that was not ending. We had come in from the balcony and there were many unfamiliar faces I had never seen. Perhaps some I might've recognized from Jacinta's photo albums of people I needed to know. I couldn't remember anyone's names for the life of me. Aiden held onto my hand. He squeezed my fingers every once in a while, and I would smile up at him. That was the only reassurance I had that I was still conscious.

All of these strangers raised their glasses to toast to us and this new monarchy that we would be creating. I sipped on my flute of champagne slowly. It was evening by the time I made it back to my room. As soon as I entered, all four of my maids shrieked, "Is our princess engaged?"

"You all knew?" I blinked at them a few times. Grace took my empty champagne flute from my hand.

"Yes. We had to make sure you looked perfect." Faith said.

Verity somberly embraced me. "You are so lucky. Is he a good kisser?"

"You all saw?" The color was draining from my face. I could feel myself go pale. Maybe this feeling was from the alcohol I drank.

They all nodded. "It is very big news. It must be on every news station."

"Thank you for making me look the part, but I have a headache again and do not wish to be disturbed. Please make my excuses to the king and queen, and the Americans."

"The Americans will be your family now too, you know." Faith's voice was melodically. "What shall we tell your fiancé?"

I turned my back to them and plopped down on the canopy bed, "You can tell him that I will see him on our wedding day."

"Ouch. I suppose that I deserve that," Aiden said in the doorway.

I sat up, not realizing he was there, standing at the corner of my room.

The maids curtsied and exited, "We will leave it to you to discuss matters then."

Aiden walked around my room, taking it all in. "Somehow, I imagined your room to have something more…" He trailed off.

"What, gold filigree and pearl encrusted furniture isn't enough for you?"

"That is not what I meant." Aiden took a seat next to me on the edge of the bed. "I was trying to say that I do not see anything of *you* in this room. Yes, it is grand, but I don't see much of your personality in it."

"I am afraid that I am not quite myself since, you know."

"I am well aware. You never used to give me the time of day before. Actually, how bad was that kiss?"

"It caught me off-guard; that's for sure," I said. I played with the lone strand of a lost bead on my gown.

"Hopefully, it was better than your first."

I didn't know what to say. Of course, Adelaide must've had lots of kisses before. For me, however, the one Aiden gave me in front of thousands of people was my first kiss ever. "Foggy memory, remember…" I tapped on my head for good measure.

Aiden grinned, "Three years ago, you kept bragging about that stupid French Prince."

"Prince Jacques?" I gave him the French prince's name, and he shook his head.

His eyes darkened, and he looked positively deadly. "The one from Monaco."

"Oh, yes, now I remember." I caught myself. I would have to do better in the future. Mixing my life and Adelaide's was getting harder and harder to keep up the facade.

"No, you don't. You have that look on your face when you think you know something, but it is so obvious that you do not. In the past week, I have gotten really good about knowing when you are lying."

"That is probably a good quality to have if you are going to be my husband."

Aiden nodded, "You have been lying an awful

lot lately."

"Let's play a game, you and I." I said to lighten the mood. "We shall ask each other questions and we must answer honestly."

Aiden perked up and seemed to enjoy this idea. "We shall start with something easy, first."

I nodded. "All right, then."

Aiden kicked off his shoes. They thudded to the floor. He crossed his legs and moved so he could face me.

I unfastened my strappy shoes and slid them onto the floor. I shifted farther onto the bed and tried to adjust my skirts so that I would not sit on them.

"Adelaide, what is your favorite tea?"

I moved slightly, trying to get more comfortable. "Really? That is what we are starting with?"

He grinned sheepishly. "You always have Earl Grey at breakfast, but I wonder if its what was given to you or if it is actually your favorite."

That was a good question. I had never had tea as fragrant as the ones I drank now. Before, Jacinta would pick some herbs and flower petals from the garden; her tea blends were a hodge-podge of whatever she could get her hands on and dry.

"Raspberry rose tea with a lot of sugar cubes is my favorite. Zachariah serves it at lunchtime. It is an afternoon-dessert tea, but I have a secret sweet tooth." I was proud of myself; the truth, for once, was out. "You're an American; do you even like tea?"

"I am only drinking it here so I could try to impress your parents. Being the American I am, I am all for the Boston Tea Party and if I could throw all of England's tea into the harbor, I would."

I laughed at that. "All except for my raspberry rose tea, I hope."

"Yes, all the tea except for your raspberry rose tea."

We bantered back and forth for quite some time. He eventually took off his suit jacket and laid back, propping his head up on one arm. He was facing me sideways.

"What is your favorite color?"

This was something that I did not know about Adelaide. This was something I did not go over as part of my sister's favorites in the lessons I had with Jacinta. Then I realized like I had before when I answered honestly about the tea question, that if I was going to become my sister and live this life and be shackled to Aiden for the good of the country, I would have to start answering everything more honestly. When in doubt, Adelaide was allowed to change her mind. "The shade of red at sunset or early morning."

"Ah, not the Tudor Red then?" He asked casually. He started tracing his fingers in circles on my arm.

I shook my head. "Nope, not quite Tudor Red. Sunset Red. How about you? Your favorite color is…?" My voice trailed off as I waited for his reply.

"Green."

"Like the color of your eyes?"

"I didn't really think about that before. I guess I do have green eyes. Wow, that makes me sound a little narcissist."

"What a pair we make … perhaps we should get married around Christmastime if our wedding colors are going to be red and green," I said jokingly.

Aiden was looking at me quite seriously.

"I wanted you to know that I had no idea about the announcement today. I only knew that my father was giving up our country, and it was merging with yours." He grabbed my hand and placed it on his chest. "Cross my heart, I did not know."

"A lot was said in that kiss of yours. You just swooped me in as soon as their eyes were on you."

"What else was I supposed to do? We were on camera and in front of the world, not just your civilians below us. Your expression was shocked, and that was not something I wanted the world to see after that announcement. I wanted everyone to see that you love me as much as I love you."

"So, you love me then?"

He leaned in close. "I know we have not seen each other in three years, but I have loved you since I set my eyes on you, since my father was vice president, and I visited during his diplomatic trips. I always made sure to visit you. Back then, though, you would never truly look twice at me. I understood then that I was not the prince you were looking for, but I hoped that if you gave me the chance, I could be the king of your heart."

"Consort."

"What?"

"You'll never be king. Apparently, anyone whom I marry will never hold a higher title than mine—even if I become queen."

"What do you mean, if? You are the only heir."

"Yes, I am," I yanked my hand off of his chest and muttered beneath my breath, "…now."

I feigned illness by putting my hand over my eyes and leaning back. I tried to hide my expression, so he could not tell whether I was lying or not. "I really *do* have a headache, though. I take it that you and your family are not leaving us tomorrow, then?"

Aiden bent down to kiss me on the forehead. "Of course not. Take as much time as you need, Adelaide."

As soon as he left my room, I broke down and cried. How was I supposed to be a princess? How was I supposed to just fall in love with someone I barely knew and had only just met? I felt more of a connection to my guard than I did to Aiden, even though we had just kissed and were now engaged.

CHAPTER
XI

I had cried for the majority of the evening. Everything was moving way too fast. I thought about how my sister would've reacted to a surprise engagement being thrust upon her. I suspected that might have been part of her mentality her whole life. She was raised with an understanding that she was a princess and would be essentially sold off to another country, to marry for a political alliance, rather than for true love. From the way that the maids and Aiden talked about her, Adelaide was friendly with her potential suitors and especially the Prince of Monaco. My sister had probably shared a hundred kisses.

In the early light of dawn, the sky was my favorite shade of red. I hadn't even bothered changing out of my blue rose dress. My maids never came back to check in on me, so it was not as if I could unbutton the snaps myself. Teeny tiny buttons trailed all along my back. The only things I was actually able to take off were my mother's tiara and the enormously long cape. Barefoot on the wooden floors, my feet barely made a sound as I slipped out of my room.

The new guard from yesterday was no longer posted at my door. There was nobody outside my room at all. That was strange. Perhaps someone had forgotten what shift they had. It gave me an ominous feeling ... like this was planned.

Officer Durant probably had the day off. He wasn't always there, but I was growing accustomed to his presence, all the same.

I did manage to dodge the patrolling guards and found myself in that little room Jacinta and I had our lessons in. I slipped into what I thought was an empty room.

Someone cleared their throat at the window. The room was dark, so I could not figure out who was there. "Tell Nico that I'll be back by my shift this evening. I just need a personal half-day to myself." He spoke, but still stared out the window.

"I am sorry, but I do not know who Nico is."

The figure turned his whole body around. "My lady, I did not realize it was you. What are you doing here? Your guard on duty should be with you." Wesley said.

I made my way closer to the window and sat next to him. "Don't you know by now that I tend to sneak out of my room a lot? My guard is not very quick on his toes." I paused and gained enough courage to tell him the next part: "He is not you."

"Are we still speaking about the other guard on duty?" Wesley asked cautiously. Perhaps he truly wanted to know what I would say. He was very direct.

I answered the question without answering him.

"Do you love him?" He asked me point blank.

"I barely know him." I answered back. It was the truth.

"You didn't answer the question." Wesley stated.

"I cannot be having this discussion with you."

My tone of voice was icier than I intended.

"Why? Is it because I am your lowly guard?" he said.

"No! Of course not. I do not dismiss people because of rank. It means nothing to me. I am not-" I stopped myself from saying *my sister*.

"You're not what?" He faced me full on. He was not going to back down.

"I am not like that." It was a poor excuse for a response, and he knew it.

He gave me a knowing look, as if he didn't believe my words.

I clarified, "I am *no longer* like that."

We sat in silence for a while. I told him that my favorite color is the red in the sky in mornings like this.

"Red sky at morning, sailors take warning." Wesley managed to say.

I finished the rhyme, "Red sky at night, sailor's delight."

"It means it'll storm today." Wesley joked. "You should not go for another boat ride."

"No, I do not believe that I will - for quite a while."

"I confess that I was angry with myself that

day. I was jealous of Aiden Smith. I felt bad that I allowed him to take you under the willow tree for a kiss and then you almost drowned."

I sucked in some air and breathed out, "You were jealous?"

"That's all you heard out of everything I just said?"

He smiled coyly, making me blush.

"Your birthday celebrations are coming up soon. I will make sure that nobody gets to you. I asked to be on your night shift from now on." He seemed to think that someone might finish what they started. "Speaking of birthdays. What is your favorite gift that anyone has ever gotten you?"

I smiled to myself. "You are going to laugh."

He gave me his pinky and promised me that he would not laugh at me, but he may laugh *with* me, however.

I held my pinky finger onto his and did not let go.

"It's not very princess-like at all. My favorite gift was a tiny pink piglet. I found him and was obsessed with the idea that he would tell me my fortune. Unfortunately, I was unable to keep him."

"I'll bet the king and queen had a fit with that. Could you imagine a pig running around the palace?" He laughed.

I sighed, realizing that my actual parents have no idea of this story. Giles and Jacinta did. I hoped that he would keep it to himself.

Wesley turned towards me in the dark and very delicately moved a strand of my hair away from my eyes.

The swift movement was so gentle, and it made me feel beautiful, like he was seeing *me,* and not Adelaide.

"What do you get the girl who has everything at her disposal?"

"Not *everything* is at my disposal." I rolled my eyes at him.

He arched his eyebrows playfully in return.

When I mustered the strength to respond, I was overcome with great sadness. I looked out the window instead, so I would not have to look him in the eyes. "We may have the world at our disposal—as you put it—but we royals can never have love … well, the unconditional kind, at least." A single tear rolled down my cheek.

I was startled when he rested his hand atop of mine. Still not looking directly at him, I leaned my head into his shoulder.

We stayed like that for a good while. Neither of us acknowledging that what we truly wanted was the one thing that neither of us could ever have.

CHAPTER XII

By the time the evening rolled around, I had made my way back to my end of the palace. I scared the maids in my room half to death. They said they almost had to tell the king and queen that I had disappeared or been kidnapped.

"I was well guarded," I assured them. "I was with Officer Durant. Now, tell me what is so urgent that you were going to alert the king and queen when you could not find me?"

The maids all looked at each other.

It was Constance that stepped forward. "It is the Prince of Monaco. He demands an audience with you."

"I am sure that my parents have already dismissed him."

"On the contrary, they want you to deal with this and send him on his way quickly. There were no royal announcements, and the public need not know about his arrival at the palace."

"I do not understand."

The maids seemed confused, but Grace spoke up. "Prince Henri Francois was your first kiss, was he not? He is ... *was* your lover? Over the past three years, I personally have sent him letters from you in secret."

"Yes, of course. How could I forget? Everything has been happening so quickly, it's making my brain hurt and its still not quite right. Do you have any of these letters from him still?"

Grace looked nervous.

"You will not be punished by any means. On my word as the princess, no harm will come to you for harboring them from me."

Grace moved over to a secret compartment in one of the elaborate dressers and handed a handful of letters to me.

"Thank you. I need to refresh my memory. If you will excuse me for an hour and then you may return to help me in a more modest gown to meet our visitor."

My maids forgot to curtsy this time. Faith said

abruptly. "That could've gone worse."

The love letters from Prince Henri Francois were tied with a black silk ribbon. It felt like I was invading my sister's privacy, but it was necessary. I had to figure out what exactly ensued between them if I were to face him. I untied the ribbon and plucked the first envelope from the stack. I soon saw that the order of the letters was a jumbled sort of mess. I was unsure what order they went in. I started to read them, anyway.

October 31st

To the girl who refuses my courtship unless I write her poetry,
The days are darkest when I am not by your side.
When we are apart, it is as if I have nearly died.
No eclipse could ever foreshadow our love.
For love itself is a gift from Heaven above.
You are the one light in my world while I am shrouded in
darkness and despair.
Yet, if you are destined to lurk in shadow; of this, I could
not bear!
I walk in the dark so that you may shine in moonlight.
You are my Northern Star that creates the brightest night.
It is Sir Shakespeare who wrote of Romeo's Juliet who is
not of the moon, but radiant as the sun.
His words are wrong! For it is the moon that shines
purely bright; its opaque beauty can never be overrun.

December 24th

To the girl who shies-away from mistletoe,

From the moment I saw you, I knew that I wanted to get to know you better. You are such a joy to be around. I am being honest with you that I did not really want to visit your country. My parents insisted that I go and do my princely duties. It was for honor that I found myself here, but it is for <u>you</u> that I find myself staying longer than I intended.

February 14th

My dearest Adelaide,

What I would do if only I could be your prince. I think about that often; you know. What it would be like to be yours truly. To be able to snuggle close to you in the morning. I'd sleep next to you when I visited, if only you would let me. I want a life with you. I intend to make you mine. Just say the three-letter word that will make all of my dreams come true, because without you I'd be living a nightmare from which I would never wake.

July 2nd

My angel ... my love,

I am not addressing you by your title. I refuse. My father is dying, and they say he will not make it through the night. I write to you that you will not be my princess, but my queen. I love you most deeply and ardently, my love. The transition of power will not be easy. My cousins have come to petition that I am unfit for the throne because "I am too English now," they say. You must meet me. If there were any way that you could outmaneuver your guards, then come to me. This way, I may show you off to the world as my queen, and none will come between us. You will be Princess of the United Kingdom, as well as Queen of Monaco.

I'd had enough of reading the prince's letters. It seemed that last letter was premature, as the King of Monaco made a full recovery two years ago. I knew that they must've really loved one another. Since I was already engaged ... *oh, wait. That is probably why the prince is here.* Two people should truly never pretend to be the same person. Things were getting out of hand.

I tossed the letters into the fireplace. If the prince really knew Adelaide, then he might know that something was wrong. It seemed like Adelaide was not close with anyone else ... or like she didn't let them see the real her. After reading her letters, I knew that she had let Prince Henri Francois see her for who she was ... just like Wesley was finally seeing me.

Adelaide might have run away with the prince and abandoned her duties, but I was not Adelaide.

~

I sat perched upon my sister's throne ... I guessed it was *my* throne now. I let the long train of my gown trail down the velvet steps. The yellow lace went all the way up my neck and down my arms. It was a very regal, modest fashion. I wanted to exude regality and power. Thick cuts of citrine gems set in rose-gold hung from my ears. It was the heaviest pair of earrings I had ever worn.

With the flick of my wrist, I motioned for the line of guards to open the doors.

Prince Henri Francois of Monaco walked in as if he owned the place. His confidence was undermining mine. He was dressed to perfection in a white crisp suit decorated with medals and ribbons, of which I did not know their meanings. A stark red cape flowed behind him. He stopped before me and bent down to one knee, lifting his head.

"Adelaide, my love, why am I the last to know that you are betrothed to someone other than myself?" His thick accent was so pronounced that his 'Ss' sounded like 'Zs'.

"You speak too formally. You forget that this is my court."

He stood up straight and moved toward the throne, but the guards lined up move closer to him. He stopped dead in his tracks. "Perhaps we can talk in private."

"This is as private as it gets. I cannot take any liberties with my safety since someone tried to kill me."

"You cannot possibly think that I ... I had nothing to do with that. Surely, you know that. You know *me.*"

"You will find that I am much changed since

the last time we spoke. My head injury has caused some memory loss."

"Have you read our letters? Do you deny our love?" He pleaded with me.

"I have read our correspondences, but those were from a different time. I am not that same person anymore."

Prince Henri Francois looked around the room. I was afraid that he would see through me. "No, I can see that clearly now," he said and turned toward the door.

I stood up from the throne and descended down the steps as he turned back and walked toward me without haste.

The guards formed a circle around us, ready to attack. I motioned for them to point their weapons toward the floor.

"Prince Henri, what are you—"

He caught me off-guard and kissed me. There was no love in the kiss at all. It was rough and desperate. I stepped back, breaking the kiss, and slapped him across the face. *Hard.* My hand buzzed with the pain of that slap.

Prince Henri Francois stood there dumbfounded. A splotch of pink appeared on his cheek where my hand was when I hit him. Then it hit me like I hit him. I just assaulted another future foreign leader.

He stared at me and then asked, "Did you truly not feel anything from that kiss?"

Without hesitation, I shook my head. "I felt nothing."

"Forgive me. I can see that now, most assuredly. You are not the Adelaide I once knew. I will leave you, and your country alone."

"Wait. I have one last favor to ask of you."

He tilted his head back. Hope sparkled in his eyes. "Anything."

"If you could please put our letters into the fire and exit discreetly, then I would be very grateful. The press has been very intrusive as of late. I would hate if our … *past* … interfered with our *separate* futures."

He bowed and left, followed by a string of guards.

CHAPTER XIII

I did not bother to change before seeing the queen. I barely had time to be announced by the guard before I burst into her suite.

She was sitting by her vanity as her lady's maid brushed her hair. She dismissed her. "Is it done then? Have you sent him away?"

I nodded. "Did you know what transpired between them?"

"No. I had my suspicions, though. I knew that Prince Henri Francois was going to be a problem if you did not take care of it yourself. Now, there is no time to delay. Your father wants you to wed before the end of the year to secure this new alliance. Apparently, there is unrest in President Smith's country, and they are not taking kindly to the news. He needs our money to pay off his country's debts, and we need his armies and resources to fend off the enemies surrounding us. We may have a strong naval base, but on land and by air, we are limited, and our family is exposed in these areas."

"You mean, me."

The queen nodded. "We have reason to believe that the assassins are angry and will try again."

"How could you possibly know that?"

"Your father and I are well-informed on the risks and threats imposed upon us. It is something that you will need to get used to when you take over for us."

"This is all happening way too fast. I'm not ready for all of this. I cannot be her."

The queen stood from the vanity chair, and I sat in it. She took the pins out of my hair and began to brush it. "Look in the mirror. What do you see?"

"My reflection."

"My dear, you look uncomfortable."

"I have never beheld my own reflection until recently. I never had any mirrors. I now understand why Jacinta told me that how I looked never mattered. It wasn't supposed to matter and if I ever saw Adelaide or our paths crossed, she told me that she hoped I would not put the puzzle pieces together."

"I was unaware of that, and I am sorry. I know that right now, when you look in the mirror, you see her, but when I look at you in the mirror, I see half of myself. Adalia, you are your own person, and you are so strong. Your time in the country has made you kind, and you have an ability to see the good in others—no matter what their station is. I am so proud of you in so many ways, and I know that this has been very difficult for you. I know that this is not a life you ever considered having, but it would make all the difference if you could try. I married your father for a political alliance, as well, but we did fall deeply in love. I think that you will make an even better monarch than your sister ever could. In many ways, she was spoiled and did not see the world the way that you do. You have such a good heart, my darling daughter. You are more suited for the royal world than you realize."

The queen took off her crown and placed it on my head.

"You are your sister in name only. Everything else is you."

During our touching mother-daughter moment, the king entered the queen's room through a secret door in the wall. It startled me. I was not expecting him to walk through the door so suddenly.

"Oh, daughter, I did not realize you were in here as well."

Still startled, I knew my eyes were widened.

The king explained, "The king and queen's suites are connected. Eventually, these rooms will be yours one day."

Queen Celine placed her hand on my shoulder. "You may keep the crown for now. It is one of many designs that will become yours soon enough. Now, be on your way. Your father and I have country matters to discuss." She added, "One more thing, I would like for you to help in planning your birthday celebrations. What would you like to do?"

"I never celebrated my birthday before. Jacinta and Giles kept that detail from me."

Her parents exchanged glances with one another. "I'll take care of it. Your birthday is on

November 27th."

Interesting. My birthday would fall on the United States holiday of Thanksgiving this year. It was a holiday that changed its date but always fell on the last Thursday of the month, a perfect birthday for an American's bride-to-be.

CHAPTER XIV

Several weeks had rolled by since the engagement and State Dinner. It was already mid-October. The leaves on the trees were beginning to change colors from verdant greens to vivid oranges and crisp reds and lemon yellows. I enjoyed the evening sunsets from my balcony at night, watching the end of day's sun rays glowing on the leaves in the gardens until it was swallowed up by the darkness of night.

Jacinta was squeezing in more royal lessons here and there. I was being asked to take on more responsibilities, of late, and I had been spending my time trying to learn how to dance gracefully.

"This is hopeless. I am absolutely terrible!" I complained.

"No, no. You are doing fine, really." Verity was lying through her teeth.

Faith was my dance partner, and she howled like a hyena every time I stepped on her toes.

I stopped to catch my breath.

Grace opened the door and grabbed my guard stationed out front inside quickly.

I turned around to see Wesley. "Officer Durant." I said and nodded my head, acknowledging his presence.

Grace shoved him towards me. "We are teaching her Highness how to waltz properly, but Faith is a terrible teacher." Grace said triumphantly.

"Oh, Grace. I don't believe its appro-" I was cut off mid-sentence.

"Actually, it may help. The rest of us are all too short to be your dance partner, Highness." I had not heard Constance enter the room until now.

Faith gave Wesley a little nudge until he crashed into me, giving me a wink. "You're not married yet, princess." She whispered discreetly so that only I could hear.

I rolled my eyes. "Fine." I took Wesley's hand in my own as he put his other hand around my waist. Verity and Faith became dance partners as well and were showing us the box step.

Constance was clapping her hands. "Marvelous! You are doing much better."

Wesley started to spin me while doing the box step so that we were actually waltzing.

The maids were giggling and having a good time. Constance and Grace even joined in.

Although we were dancing, I tried not looking at Wesley. He kept his face stone-like, too. We had not had the chance to talk since that night I found him in the unused room of the West Wing. He had been changing his shifts a lot. I had been told that he guarded my room in the middle of the night, which is why he was not there to escort me during the day. The last time I saw him was when I had an audience with the Prince of Monaco. He was, unfortunately, one of the guards in the room that day. He saw the kiss between Prince Henri Francois and me.

Wesley waltzed me over to the open doors of my balcony.

"I feel as though you are avoiding me." I said to him. I was doubtful that my maids could hear our conversation above their laughter.

He finally looked down at me, meeting my

eyes. "I am simply doing my duty. Nico has changed my shifts is all."

"Is that due to the schedule of the guards or because you asked him to?"

Without warning, he dipped me so low to the ground I thought he was going to drop me. When I came back to an upright position, he answered me. "I asked. I thought it was best if I kept my distance."

"What if your future sovereign demands that you be reinstated at my door during the day, to perform your escorting duties?"

Wesley smiled faintly. "Then I will do as my lady commands."

"Wesley, that's not what I meant. It was not an order."

He dipped me again, but this time, it was slower. Our faces were inches apart. His blue-green eyes went from my eyes to my mouth, and I thought he was going to kiss me. Honestly, part of me wanted him to. I had been kissed by Aiden Smith and by Prince Henri Francois, but Wesley Durant was the one I most ached for. My heart skipped a beat.

But as soon as it almost happened, it was

over. The door to my room was flung open, and Jacinta stood in the doorway. Wesley brought me up from our dip. He moved away from me as fast as it took Jacinta to cross the room.

Wesley bowed before me and then resumed his post outside my open doors.

Jacinta watched him as he left. "My dear, you must tread carefully with that one."

"Whatever do you mean?" I sighed and went to grab my glass of water.

My maids had left us, as well, most likely to grab us some lunch. For the moment, it was just Jacinta and me.

She whispered, "You forget sometimes who raised you. I know you, Dahlia."

"What is that supposed to mean?" I took a sip of the ice-cold water.

"I have been watching you closely, even here at the palace. You look at your guard in the way you should be looking at the one you are betrothed to."

"That's not..."

Jacinta raised her hand. I knew better than to talk over her when she was like this. She wanted to be heard out so I would let her.

"Whatever is happening there, I do not want to know about it."

"Nothing has happened!" My voice was raised higher than it should.

"Good." Jacinta said sternly and then gave me a look as if she did not believe me.

I assured her. "Nothing will happen."

"That is what I wanted to hear. You are no longer my flower. For all intents and purposes, your actions reflect upon crown and country—especially when you become queen."

"That is very far off. I can assure you."

"It might not be that far off as you may think."

Dread filled my veins. My stomach fell. "Why? What do you know?"

"I can say nothing right now. I just hear things that I should not. I am concerned for you, that's all."

"Don't be. As I said, nothing is going on there."

"Then do not give him hope where there is none. From what I could see, there is hope in his eyes for you. You need to shut it down."

Every word was emphasized in her last sentence to me.

I smiled, changing the subject as my maids came in with hot soup, biscuits and tea for lunch. "Shall we take our tea, then?" I asked Jacinta as if we were just chatting about trivial things such as the weather.

My maids stilled. They curtsied at the open doorway.

"Please do not mind me. I just wish to say my goodbyes to my fiancée." Aiden was standing in the doorway.

"Of course." Jacinta said as she beckoned the maids to leave out the service doors.

I had been avoiding Aiden and making excuses in the past week not to see the Americans, either. I had turned down two invitations to tea with Lady Irene already. By the third attempt, I would eventually have to cave. I mean, if everything continued the way it had been, she would be my mother-in-law after all.

Aiden left the door open. "I heard that you were practicing for the masquerade at the end of the month."

"Yes, I wanted to perfect the waltz, seeing as we will be dancing it together to open the ballroom floor for other couples," I said.

"I thought that our parents were going to be opening the dance floor?" Aiden asked.

"It would appear that they are passing the torch to us."

He stared at the floor. "That changes the timeline on things a bit."

"The timeline for what?" I was curious.

He shrugged.

"Aiden?" I asked, but he looked distant.

He still said nothing.

"Aiden Valentine, answer me." I said in my most regal tone.

That jolted him out of his thoughts. "Gosh, that was scary. You reminded me of my nanny from when I was a kid. Anytime I misbehaved, she would call me that and I knew I was in trouble." Aiden said, remembering fondly.

I folded my arms across my chest. "You were saying that the masquerade ball is messing up your timeline."

"I meant nothing by that."

"No, tell me." My tone was more forceful.

Aiden shook his sandy blonde hair. The length of it was reaching above his eyes. It made him look younger. He stepped forward and wrapped his arms around me.

I returned his embrace. "Aiden, is everything all right?"

He pulled apart from me, but my arms were still around the back of his neck.

"Adelaide, no matter what happens, I want you to know that I do love you. I meant every word that I had said before. I've loved you from the moment I saw you all those years ago."

He was staring at me like he was waiting for me to say something. He had just poured his heart out to me, but I did not know what to say.

"I do care for you, but everything is happening so fast. We have only just met and…"

"No, we haven't." Aiden wriggled out from our hug and my arms.

Crap! Every time I try and be honest, it backfires. "What I meant is that it *seems* like we have only just met." I was flustered now. The words I should be saying were dry on my tongue. I could not keep catching myself. I was torn in two directions, and I did not know how much longer I could keep up this charade. Random sounds that were the start of words escaped from me. They were almost robotic and did not make sense.

Aiden tried to go in for a kiss, but at the last second, I turned so that he pressed his lips to my cheek instead. We had not kissed since the announcement of our engagement. After his declaration of love, I could not kiss him in this moment. My heart was somewhere else. It was not fair to him, even though it would be expected of us to play the infatuated love birds sooner or later.

When he pulled back from my cheek, he bowed and said, "I will wait for your feelings to catch up with mine. My father was adamant that we set our wedding date by the end of the year. It seems that my father's cabinet members are pressing him that our alliance is set in stone before he absolves the Presidency. Things are not going well on my side of the pond."

I was taking in everything he said. Of course, it was not enough that we signed a peace treaty at the State Dinner. A piece of paper could be ripped up, and Oliver Smith did not want to get burned. It would cost him more than it would cost this monarchy; that was for certain. He wanted this wedding to be a done deal to make the alliance permanent.

"I see. Are we to have our Christmas wedding, after all?" I said, mildly joking.

"This is serious, Adelaide. Even returning home right now with my family is putting us in danger. There are riots in the streets. I am unsure whether my people want to be ruled by a monarchy again. It took over 100 years for my country to establish its independence from yours. Now, it's like it was all for nothing. My father seems to have thought that the people would rally behind us, and we would have peace, but that can only happen if the people believe that this were a love match and not necessarily for the political advantages that our union would bring."

I had nothing to say to that. Aiden was putting everything on the line for a person whom he didn't even know. Part of me wondered if he were really here for Adelaide or just for his father's ambitions. What would Adelaide have done if she were in this situation? Would she have become princess, or Queen of Monaco? Or would she have done what was expected of her at home? Furthermore, if I were still living my carefree life in the country with Giles and Jacinta, then who would I have married?

"I will be gone for a few weeks," he continued. "I plan to return in time for the masquerade ball. Hopefully, that will give you some time to think about ... everything. By then, I believe that both of our parents will want to have a date set."

I nodded. There was really nothing left for me to say.

Aiden left my room, and I sat outside on my balcony, contemplating my choices. I had not truly accepted my fate as princess yet. Was there really no way out of this for me?

CHAPTER
XV

In the days that followed Aiden and his family's departure, I could not help but wonder … what if they never returned? Even if they didn't, I was not so sure that I would be free to wed someone whom I cared about. Jacinta's words kept creeping into the crevices of my mind: *You look at your guard in the way you should be looking at the one you are betrothed to.*

It seemed that no matter what happened when the Americans approached their government with the new changes and the peace treaty, I was stuck playing a pawn in everyone else's game. Well, I was done being a lowly pawn. I decided that I was going to be the queen on the chessboard, and queens could move however they pleased.

It took a few days, but Wesley Durant eventually switched his shifts back to daytime hours. I had him escort me everywhere I went, which consisted of the Great Hall and the West Wing and, occasionally, the gardens. Life at the palace had died down again without anyone staying with us currently. In a few weeks, however, we were going to have a hundred guests from all corners of the world staying with us for the masquerade ball at the end of the month.

I had helped to design the invitations that were already sent. Yesterday, I had met with the chefs and to taste all kinds of delicate dishes and fine wines for the event. It was going to be fantastic, especially the desserts.

Today, though, there was nothing special planned. Jacinta had not scheduled anymore lessons with me, with all the hustle and bustle of planning the masquerade. Even my maids were busy sewing my gown and hand-making my mask. They told me that I was not allowed to see it until it was finished.

They were also asked by the queen to make costumes for the guards. Apparently, the masquerade was one of few events in which the palace staff could dress up and attend in shifts.

Not knowing with whom one was speaking added a little pizzazz. It could have been a servant—or even the king himself!

I had been walking in circles and Wesley knew it. Although, he did not say one word about it. I had not yet taken his arm and was keeping my distance a bit. Not so much that I thought he was the living plague, but enough to keep myself from pesky thoughts of his hands and how they felt around my waist when we danced. I bit my bottom lip, deep in thoughts I should not be daring to think about.

Finally, he broke the silence. "My lady, would you like me to lead you in a direction? I know the entire palace by heart and could practically walk it even in my sleep."

"Hmmm. That is odd."

"What is, my lady?" He asked as we stopped.

"Just that I have seen no guards patrolling in a while. It is strange because they're always around a corner. Now with the Smiths gone, I'd think that there would be even more guards left to spare for extra protection at the perimeters of the palace."

Wesley removed my hand from his arm and

went for his weapon.

Before he could respond, something shattered the windows behind us.

We were on the fourth floor. A metal ball spewed smoke out of its side and clanged to the ground, rolling in front of our feet. Wesley's soldier instincts kicked in and he gripped my shoulder fiercely, moving us down the hallway so fast I could hardly keep up. In the next moment, Wesley shoved me against the wall.

"Don't move." He ordered, panting down my neck. He slammed into me, covering me with himself.

The glass sounded as if it broke into a thousand pieces. Wesley shielded me. He grunted and then peeled me off the wall. We sprinted around the corner so fast. I lost my shoes and was running barefoot on the broken shards of glass. I'd rather have my feet sliced open than the horrific alternative.

The scene before us was pure chaos. There were palace guards with and without their jackets on. Each side was firing at the other. I could not tell who was whom. From the looks of it, neither could Wesley.

A guard still with his crimson jacket on shouted, "They've broken our perimeter! Get her Highness to safety!"

A set of a dozen guards without their jackets on marched towards the ones with jackets from down the hall.

Wesley grabbed my hand. "See that staircase fifty feet from us?"

I nodded, too scared to speak.

"On three, we are going to run over there. One … two … *three!*"

The two sets of guards were firing their weapons. Bullets streamed through the air. Candelabras folded upon themselves. Tapestries moved as if a servant were beating out the dust. Holes in the walls remained.

We ran like our lives depended on it. It was a miracle we weren't struck down.

As soon as the thought entered my mind, pain shot through my hand, breaking the grasp that I'd had on Wesley's. We had made it to the stairwell, but not without a price to pay. Blood was dripping from both our hands. A bullet had made a clean shot through our embrace. Neither of us were spared.

I held my hand to my chest and kept running. We made it up the winding staircase to the fifth floor—the tower rooftop.

Wesley and I caught our breaths for a moment. He checked the small hallway for guards without jackets. Whoever was behind this attack, they had infiltrated our staff and disguised themselves with their uniforms. An edge of the stone wall crumbled near Wesley's head.

"Snipers! Go!" Wesley shouted and pushed me closer to the ground. "Across the walkway there is a floor-length painting. Behind the painting is a door to a secret passageway. No matter what happens, you get to that door. Do you hear me?"

"I am not leaving you!" I cried out. We did not have time to argue. Bullets flew right above our heads.

Wesley fell to his knees, crying out in pain on the way down. He put his good hand to his left side. He had been hit. I yanked him until he was next to me. We crawled over to where he said there would be the painting.

Echoes of footsteps running up the stairs

were heard. Guards, good or bad, were coming up to this floor. We would be caught in the crossfire again.

My bloody hand reached to the side of the painting, and I pulled it as hard as I could. The entire portrait ripped off the side of the wall to reveal a door. I tore it open, and we crashed inside. I closed the door, which sealed with a metal clank.

Behind me I heard a click and there was a lightbulb that dimly lit the cramped enclosure. Wesley was on all fours in the middle of the room. His hand pressed into his side.

"What if they try to open the door?" I asked frantically. The pain in my hand was becoming more and more unbearable as my adrenaline waned.

It is eerily quiet inside this room.

Wesley was breathing heavily. "Only ... can be ... opened from inside once it's been occupied." Every breath he took was ragged.

"Wesley." I moved next to him and helped him onto his back.

He sucked in a breath and grunted. "Check ... for supplies."

I went to my feet and looked around the room. It was the size of a small bedroom. There was a sink and a shelf with blankets, some cans of food, and a metal container. I grabbed the container and a blanket, bringing it over to Wesley in the middle of the space, and opened the metal box. Inside there were first aid supplies.

Wesley moved his bloody hand to cup my face. "Are you hurt?" He asked with such sincerity.

"Just my hand, and not nearly as badly as you."

His hand moved from my face to my bad hand, which lay limp at my side. He grabbed the bottle of disinfectant and poured it over both our hands.

I squeezed my eyes shut and bit the inside of my cheek.

Without saying anything, I allowed Wesley to wrap our hands with thick gauze. Luckily for me, the bullet hole was in the space in between my thumb and index finger. I did not think my wound broke through bone. Just flesh. Unfortunately for Wesley, his wound was gaping in the middle of his left hand.

He bobbed his head. Wesley was fighting consciousness.

I grabbed his face in my hands.

His head fell back.

"No. No. No. No. No. Wes!" I shook him hard.

No response.

"Wes, wake up!" I screamed.

His eyes fluttered. "Not … so loud."

"You are losing too much blood. I need to see your side." I tried to stay as calm as I could.

His whole jacket was soaked black with blood.

I grabbed the blanket, rolled it up, and put it behind his head for a pillow. I grabbed him underneath his armpits and dragged him into a slumped, upright position. I went around him and took off his jacket slowly. The jacket was heavy from the weight of the blood. I laid him back down gently.

I unbuttoned his shirt and peeled it off his side. I went back to the sink and wet some rags that were by the blankets and came back down to tend to his wound. I must have gone through all the rags we had in order to soak up the blood that came flowing from his side. Nothing I did was helping.

"I will walk … you … walk you through … what you need t-t-to do." Wesley barely got through the words.

"All right. What do I do next?"

"Find the bullet. Is … is there a suture kit?" he asked.

I searched the container and found what he was asking for. "Yes, I think this is it." I put a glove on my good hand. "This is going to hurt. A lot."

Wesley nodded.

I put my fingers in his side. It was gooey like the inside of a pastry filled with fruit preserves. I felt something solid and hard. "I think I feel it!"

I took out my hand and got the tweezers. I reached back inside the wound until I felt it again. I opened the tweezers and toggled them until I was certain that I had the bullet. Wesley's legs twitched. His face was contorted.

I went back up to the shelf and washed off my glove in the sink. There had to be something that would help the pain. I spotted a bottle with amber liquid in the back behind the cans of food. Ah ha! I opened the bottle and took a big whiff of it. Whatever kind of alcohol this was, had to have been strong. It smelled like it's been aging a long time in this secret room.

"Here, drink this." I lifted the bottle to his mouth and tipped it. He took three large gulps, and I took the bottle. I tipped it back and downed a few large sips myself.

"You're going to … need to stitch … me up," he managed to say.

I took the needle and sutures. It's like sewing a patch on a piece of cloth. I kept telling myself that his skin was really just fabric. I had become an excellent liar in the past two months. I almost believed myself too. That it was not a living, breathing person under my needle, but a pile of blankets in need of sewing repair.

By the time I had finished and cut the thread, Wesley had drifted off. I removed my glove and closed the lid on the box of supplies.

I put my head on his chest, hovering over him. His heart was still beating, and his chest slowly rose and deflated. I tried to move, but I felt pressure on my back. His arm had willed me into place. I adjusted, laying my head in the crook of his arm. I curled against his unwounded side.

I had saved him, and I permitted myself to rest for a while. If we were the only ones who could open the door from within the secret room, then our best bet to stay alive was to wait for the attack to end.

~

I awoke gasping for air. In my dream, I was drowning, surrounded by darkness. In the dimly lit room, there were no windows. No tunnels. No way to tell how much time had passed. Warmth filled me. I was overheating, actually. I lifted my head and saw that I was still beside Wesley. He was conscious now.

"My lady, are you all right?"

I looked up at him. "I could be better. Bad dream. Do you think that everyone else made it to safety?"

"I do not know. I am hopeful that they did. If anything, I have done my job. You are safe and that is all that matters."

"Because I am the heir." I muttered. My hand was throbbing in pain.

"Adelaide."

I tightened up upon hearing her name. I hated that my sister's name was spoken so tenderly from upon his lips.

"Surely, you can see that even though you are the heir to the throne, it does not matter to me. I see *you*. I wanted to rescue you because I … I care for you. You are important to me, and not because you wear a crown or sit on a throne. I…" He caught himself.

"Go on … I need to hear the rest of it."

"I should not be saying these things to you."

"If what you say, about me being a royal not meaning anything to you, then please say the rest. I want to hear it. I need to hear it." I sat up so that I could look at Wesley in the eyes.

He raised his good hand up to my face and caressed my cheek. I leaned into his touch.

He spoke. "I care for you. Deeply. It runs past my desire to protect you as your guard. I see you not as my sovereign, but as something more."

Before he could say anything else, I brought my face down to his and our lips touched in a light and gentle kiss. I leaned myself into him. He brought his good hand down my neck, trailing down my sides. I parted my mouth and felt the tip of his tongue as the kiss deepened. I played with the dark tendrils of his hair that wisped on the back of his neck.

When we finally broke the kiss, we were both breathing heavily. I lay back down and nestled close to his side. I was in a cocoon of happiness for the time being. Our bandaged hands locked onto each other. We stayed like that until we drifted off to sleep.

CHAPTER
XVI

I awoke to the sound of banging on the secret room door. Wesley slept soundly next to me. I wasn't sure if it was someone good or bad on the other side of the door. I grabbed Wesley's weapon and pointed it at the door before opening it to find four guards with jackets on.

"Whoa, princess! Put the gun down. It's all right now. The assassins are gone."

I kept the weapon pointed straight at them. "How do I know that you are not one of them in our guard's clothing?"

The young man before me put down his own gun and held out his hands up in the air. Another guard came into view behind him and it's the one I recognized from when Wesley took his days off.

I dropped my weapon upon seeing him and wept. The guard put his weapon away and asked if I was hurt anywhere.

"My hand, but I'll be fine. Officer Durant is the one that needs a doctor." I pointed to him from within the room. Wesley was still sleeping or unconscious. It was most likely the latter of the two.

The other three guards rushed into the room and helped Wesley to his knees. They dragged him out of the secret room and almost carried him all the way to the infirmary. In the light of day, I could see the gore of my blood-stained gown. I could see why the guard thought I was severely injured. Most of it was from when I was kneeling in Wesley's blood, trying to stitch up his side.

The guard looked horrified at me. "Why is Officer Durant in that state?"

"He saved my life by taking me to safety. He took a bullet for me. I stitched him up in that room so he would not bleed out. I did the best that I could, but I have no idea if he sustained any major internal damage."

The guards exchanged glances with one another. They helped Wesley onto one of the few empty white infirmary cots. There were so many people occupying the space. It was better that they were alive and there. I had also seen the stack of dead bodies that did not make it through the attack on the palace.

Peeking out from the doorway were Constance, Faith, and Verity. My maids all embraced me in a huddle.

I pulled them off to the side, away from prying ears.

"Where is Grace?" I asked, worried.

Faith and Verity burst into tears.

Constance replied, "She never made it to one of the safe rooms. She is … Your Highness, Grace is dead."

I brought my bandaged hand to my lips, covering my mouth. "No. How could this happen?"

"Grace was supposed to be meeting with someone. She said it was important. I thought she might be doing something for you, Highness. Shortly after, we heard the gunshots up above and I motioned others to follow me to our safe rooms in the servant's quarters."

I shook my head. "Grace was not doing anything for me. Who could she have been meeting with?"

Constance, Faith, and Verity all looked at one another. No one knew whom or why, but I was determined to find out what she was doing when she died.

"Your Highness." A short, brunette-haired nurse, dressed in white, approached us.

I nodded to my maids to leave us.

Each of them curtsied and left.

I turned to the nurse. "Yes?"

"May I?" she asked, gesturing to my bandaged hand. It looked to be about the size of an oven mitt.

I held out my hand for her to examine. She unwrapped it and tended to it.

I hadn't really taken a look at my hand until now. It was quite gruesome. The space between my thumb and index finger was completely torn through. The wound still bled slowly, but it was better than before. I looked around the infirmary. Too many beds were being used up. So many curtains were opening and closing for newly admitted people. It was chaos.

"The king and queen, are they all right?" My voice wavered.

"Yes. Both of them were boarded up in their suites. I sent one of the less-injured guards to inform them that you were found safe." She replied.

I lowered my voice for the request that I was about to make. Since I was the princess, I knew it was something that she could not refuse. "I would like a list of the names of those who gave their lives today. Please send it with whoever is on duty to guard my room tonight."

She nodded as she finished up with my hand. "I will, your Highness. Give me an hour and the list will be with you. I will be discreet."

"Thank you. It is appreciated."

She bowed her head to me and left to tend to other patients.

Before I could leave, I had to see Wesley one more time to make sure he was all right. I was upset that he had not woken up when they dragged him all the way there. I flung open the curtains of the room where the guards had taken him. Nobody was there. The bedcovers were tossed to one side.

"Durant's not there." Someone informed me from behind.

I whirled around and saw a dark-haired guard. It was one of the ones who had helped carry him there.

"Where was he taken?" I asked.

Please let him be all right. I hope that I did not injure him more with my bad stitching skills.

"Nurse said he needed surgery. They took him away on a cot with wheels."

I nodded and found a guard waiting for me at the end of the line of infirmary beds. We walked in silence back to my room.

~

My maids undressed me and took my ruined dress away. They would most likely dispose of it. I would not mind. It's not like I would ever wear it again. Constance and Verity scrubbed me down, trying to wash away all the dirt and caked blood in my hair and underneath my fingernails.

After they dried me off and fit me into a little lace nightgown, Faith entered with a piece of paper next to my teacup saucer. She slipped it under there so quietly that the other two maids did not notice. She made sure that I made eye contact with her before she left again.

I sent Constance and Verity away shortly after. I picked up the saucer and unfolded the small piece of paper. It was a list of names of the fallen staff members in the palace.

I did not recognize any of the names until I reached the bottom of the page. Jacinta and Giles. I cried out and fell to my knees.

The guard outside my room hurtled through the double doors, weapon at the ready. He halted when he saw me on the floor.

"Your Highness. Do you need any assistance?" He said as he helped me to my feet.

My eyes were wet. I knew that it was improper to cry in front of others and to show such emotion, but I simply could not help myself. I did not want to be the princess right now. If Jacinta and Giles were gone, then I truly had nobody to whom I could confide about anything anymore. Besides the king and queen, no one else at the palace knew of the deceit that I was a part of, pretending to be my sister.

The guard cleared his throat. "Faith ran into one of the nurses. She had a message that she wanted delivered to you. I know that you placed your trust in her, as well as your maid. I would not break it for the world and wanted to let you know that I will be discreet with this knowledge as well."

I nodded. "What news do you have?"

"Durant is undergoing surgery right now. Your stitching skills were good, but when the doctors opened up your sutures to check the insides … it seems the bullet did some damage internally."

"I took the bullet out. It did not break."

"I know. Between us, one of the guards told the doctor that it was them that took out the bullet, after you both were found. He thought it would be better for you that way, seeing as Durant was partially disrobed."

"I see. Thank you for that. Will he, will Officer Durant live?" I held my breath.

He nodded.

I exhaled. "Good. Thank you for the message."

"Your Highness. I will be just outside if you need anything. Please do not hesitate to call on me."

CHAPTER
XVII

The next morning, I hesitated before exiting my room. Constance had informed me that Verity had resigned as my lady's maid. She felt that, after the attack on the palace, no one was safe anymore. Verity mentioned that I needed to watch my back and be careful whom I trusted. I was not sure whether those were supposed to be words of wisdom or a blatant threat. I'd never truly figured out how good of a liar Verity was. Of course, that was not the official story of why she left. Apparently, she needed to "return home to be with her family."

When Constance left the room, my temporary guard opened my doors, as I was not ready to leave for the day. He came over and set a tiny note on my vanity and left.

The note said:

> *Surgery was a success. Alive and well.*
> *Asking for you.*

I tossed it into the fire and made sure that it burned before I left. Today would not be easy. I was meant to be on a live video broadcast to demonstrate to the world that the British Monarchy was still alive—despite the second attack. The king and queen made a rare television appearance every so often. They usually had other speakers give speeches and make statements for them.

The papers were ablaze with the tragedy at the palace. The king and queen were dressed in their finest, with their crowns atop their heads. They came towards me and drew me into a group hug.

"I am truly very sorry about the Lockwoods. I know how important they were to you. Their service will not be in vain. You are alive, thanks to their efforts."

I pulled back from my parents' embrace.

"What do you mean, I am alive because of them?"

The queen put a hand to my face and sadly smiled. "They held off many of the intruders and were the first ones to sound the alarm when they did not recognize one of the guard's faces. They knew everyone who worked at the palace. My lady's maid told me that we should be wary of guards with an X tattoo. It was their symbol. That is how they knew each other, and whom to trust."

My guard. The few times that Wes was trying to change his shifts. There was a guard with an X tattoo on his neck. But, if the guard was meant to kill me, why did he not when he had ample opportunities to do so? What changed? What was he waiting for?

One of the staff members who was in the broadcasting room in the palace shouted out, "Five minutes, everybody!"

The queen patted my cheek. "Adelaide, are you all right?"

I was pulled back from my realization. After this, I would have to see if it was true. My stomach turned sour. I wanted to be anywhere but on video right now.

I pulled back the curtain and took my place next to the king and queen in the middle of the room. There were at least a dozen cameramen, each taking shots of us from different angles.

King Cassian started the announcement. "We have some sad news to share today. As I am sure everyone knows by now, there was a second attack on the palace. Although the queen, our daughter Princess Adelaide, and I are unharmed, many of our loyal staff members did not make it through."

As the king's speech went on, and he read the list of the deceased, I could not focus. By the time he read Jacinta and Giles' names, I had almost lost it. The tears sprang forth as if my eyes were a clogged aqueduct, ready to explode. I could not read any statements today. Instead, I ran offstage.

The only place I wanted to be was also the only place I was dreading visiting. The infirmary had been a place of chaos, but now it seemed more a place of peace and resting. That, or everyone who hadn't been cleared to leave was sedated. I moved from cot to cot but did not find who I was looking for.

It was strange to be walking alone in the palace, especially after everything that had happened. I spotted Zachariah opening one of the servant's quarter doors. They were hidden skillfully. He saw me and bowed. "Your Highness, is there anything you require?"

"Actually, yes. I need you to show me the guards' rooms. There is someone I need to see."

He hesitated. "I am unsure if that is wise-"

I cut him off. "You will show me now. That is an order from your future sovereign."

Zachariah glared at me but opened the door wider for me to fit through. "I am obligated to tell their Majesties about this."

"I am sure you are." I spat back.

We moved through the servants' quarters hastily. There was a whole labyrinth of hallways and staircases. They must've been adjacent to the hallways of the palace, but these were specially designed for the staff to not be seen. I wondered, if I were not born to the king and queen but to Giles and Jacinta, would I have worked with them at the palace? Would I have been the invisible one on these sides of the walls?

"Down this staircase, make a left. The guard's rooms are sanctioned there. To the right are the rooms of the male butler, valets, chauffeurs, and others of similar titles. I suggest that you are not seen by anyone else, your Highness. Gossip amongst people such as myself is all we have. Some are willing to even pay for what they know."

"Are you one of those kinds of people, Zachariah?"

I shut my eyes, waiting for an answer that was never spoken. When I opened my eyes, he was gone.

I made my way down the stairs to the left, as instructed. I read the names off the plaques on each of the doors. *P. Durant.* I stopped as I saw the unfamiliar name. Did Wesley have a brother? I opened the door.

The guards' quarters were not what I thought they were. I found myself in a small, cramped room. There was hardly enough space for a bed and a small wardrobe and a mirror. I closed the door behind me.

"I was not expecting to see you for a while." Wesley purred.

He was lying in bed, propped up by two pillows behind him. He was shirtless, but the lower half of his torso was bandaged with white tape and gauze that stopped just below his pecs.

"We need to talk." I said, as I folded my arms across my chest.

"That is the four-word death sentence that no man wants to hear." He struggled to sit higher.

"Were you aware that the guard who was stationed outside my room while you tried to change your shifts was one of those who could have killed me in this attack?" I asked directly.

Wesley wrinkled his forehead. "Grigori was a part of this? How would I have known that?"

"So you knew him by name. Why does your door say P. Durant, Wesley?"

"P. is the initial of my first name, but I never go by it," he said.

"You told me your name was Wesley. Is everything out of your mouth been a lie this entire time?" My voice was bitter.

"No. Not everything." He moved and winced. He motioned for me to sit next to him, but I did not move.

He continued. "My name is Phelan Wesley Durant. I do not use my first name."

"Whatever this was between us must end. You can blame it on a moment of weakness, or a near death experience in the safe room if you want. You can blame it on the liquor we shared while I stitched you up."

"What we have is real. I may not be a prince—"

"The point is you are not my betrothed. He is not a prince, either, but I gave him my word that we would be married. We have signed a peace treaty stating such."

"You would still go through with that now after everything that has happened?" He asked, upset.

"Shhh! Else you are going to draw attention to this room." I shushed him.

"It was more than the safe room. You know that. You kissed me, remember? Or are you going to blame it on your head injury too, like you do everything else?" Wesley shouted venomously.

"Stop trying to point everything back to me!"

I raised my voice a little higher this time.

"How can I not when everyone is riding on your every word? You can make or break any alliance by just being you. You have the power here. Not I. Not Smith. Not even the prince whom Grace kept secret from everyone else. I have been in the palace for a few years, princess. You forget that everyone below the royal status talks about and sees things they're not meant to," Wesley said.

"Speaking of Grace. She died trying to visit someone in the palace. Did you see her before then?"

"How was I supposed to see her? I was with you the entire time. Or have you forgotten that as well? I took a blasted bullet in the side for you!"

I looked from his angry face to his torso. "Explain Grigori to me." I demanded.

"If you have been in the palace as a guard for years, as you said, how did you not know that Grigori was a new face amongst the guard?"

"I've known Grigori for years." Wesley's eyes looked away from me now.

"How?" I demanded from him.

"What?"

"How do you know the guard? And *do not lie to me,*" I said intensely.

"We are both guards. How else would I know him?"

"Wrong answer. I know about the tattoos. I know that the ones who wore them were the ones that wanted me dead. Grigori had it on his neck in plain sight for anyone to see." The more that I spoke, the more that Wesley's eyes darkened. The fear spreading across his features like wildfire. "Explain to me that the tattoo is not one that matches the others that fell. Explain to me why he was on my shift when you were not there. Explain something believable to me."

He stared at me. "I can't." He whispered so softly I almost did not hear it.

"If I order you to take off your bandages. Will I see edges of a similar tattoo? It did not hit me then, when I was drenched in your own blood, trying to save your life. Are you part of the people that tried to kill me?" I asked point blank. There was no return now.

"Do you remember when you saw me in the

gardens?"

"You'll have to be more specific. I've seen you in the gardens a lot in the last three months."

"The first time when I crawled up the ivy."

"You had your weapon out." I paused. "I told you to put your dagger away because I was safe."

He nodded. "It was strange to me that Grigori insisted that he had killed you. That you would have the scars. That you were dead."

Grigori was the one that killed my sister.

Wesley continued. "I was sent to finish the job. I knew the palace inside and out. I would have made it quick. That night on the balcony, I knew that you were different. That you really did not remember who you were before. What you were willing to do to this country. All in the name of love, apparently. You would have died for it, had anyone else known."

"So, you admit it. That you are a part of the group that tried to have me assassinated. Twice!" I clenched my good hand at my side. My gloves helped to hide the wound in my hand.

"It may have started out that way. But you were different. You were not going to throw away everything and destroy this country anymore. I knew it from the moment you sent Prince Henri Francois packing, that you had indeed changed. That you were no longer a threat."

"A threat to whom?"

"I'll chalk it up that you truly do not remember what you were going to do after your injuries." Wesley pointed out.

I stood there, dumbfounded. What was Adelaide going to do that would involve the destruction of the country?

"I told Grigori that the plot was off. That everyone needed to disappear as if they never existed at the palace to begin with. Then there were a few loyal ones that worked at the palace for so long that they were recognizing who we all were. They had to be eliminated."

"All the people on that list that my father is reading their names, all knew that my life was in danger?"

"Not all of them. Some got in the way. Casualties; nothing more."

"That does not explain why you were shot."

"I betrayed my comrades in arms. I protected you when I was ordered to kill you instead." He shrugged.

How could I have been so stupid? I would have given up everything to someone who was going to stab me in the back. Literally.

"Who ordered you to kill me, and why?"

"I cannot reveal that, but I will tell you that Grace, your maid, read all the letters that went back and forth between you and the Prince of Monaco. She reported the letter's contents back to certain sources. You were going to absolve the monarchy. You were going to leave this country without leadership. All to elope with the prince when his father was in critical condition. The two of you were going to fake your deaths and go off the grid together. You both were going to leave your countries in ruin. Do you know what would have happened to the whole of Europe?"

It would have been chaos. It would be like what Aiden was describing about what was happening in his own country.

"Your plan is ridiculous. Even if the attempts

on my life were successful, this country would still be in chaos. There would be no monarchy and no leadership left if I were eliminated—unless someone else was going to take the throne ... but who?"

Wesley confessed, "I did some digging. The monarchy funded a remote little estate somewhere in Wales. I hired someone to take pictures of it, but it was abandoned a few months ago. Whomever or whatever the king was using that space for was gone. Everything vanished with it. If only I had gotten there a few weeks earlier, then perhaps I would have figured out why. My gut feeling says that King Cassian had a child out of wedlock and was keeping them alive. If that were true, then we were going to put this child on the throne. I was plotting and trying to find where they moved whoever was living in that country estate, while Grigori insisted that I let him guard your room."

"You trusted him enough to watch me when he had already killed me once before?"

"Killed you?" He asked unsteadily.

"That did not come out the way I intended it

to." There couldn't be any backpedaling. I could not explain this, but neither could I explain that King Cassian was always faithful to his queen, that there was no child born out of wedlock ... just one that was not meant to exist. After all that was said tonight, I could never trust Wesley again. I'd take the secret of my existence and the real Adelaide's death to my grave.

"What did you mean to say exactly?" Wesley shifted, trying to get out of the bed.

"If you are not gone by the end of the day, I will personally have you arrested and hung for the attempted murder of your future queen."

"Adelaide!"

"That's not my name!" I shouted back, not caring who heard.

CHAPTER XVIII

Phelan Wesley Durant vanished by the end of the day. When the nurses came to check in on him, there was nothing left behind. Not even his old used bandages. It was like he never existed at all.

Grigori was also gone, as well as a dozen other staff members all ranging in titles that were in close proximity to me and their Royal Majesties, my parents. It would seem that when Wesley exited, so did the looming threat over the palace.

It was such a betrayal knowing the truth now. Even though I now know what happened to my sister. What she was willing to do. The secrets everyone was keeping. It was all out in the open, but I realized after the anger wore off that it did not matter. Nothing would have changed. No number of wishes or prayers could bring Adelaide back. She was dead.

This entire time, I had been living in her shadow. It was time to step into the light. I was at a point where I could no longer pretend to be her, but that did not mean I had to give up the secret. I may wear her face, but inside I was Adalia. Inside, I was still me.

Jacinta was right all along. I may not have been born first, but I decided that I would no longer act like I was in second place, either. The time had come for me to embrace my future. I was not going to hold back any longer.

By the end of the week, Aiden Smith returned to the palace, unaccompanied by his parents. There was no welcoming party of the staff or big announcement like there had been before. I almost preferred it that way. The only difference was where Aiden's luggage went to. Apparently, he had told Zachariah to take his belongings somewhere in the West Wing. Close to where what was supposed to be my temporary rooms were, but not so close - or even on the same floor - so not to cause a scandal. I never did move into Adelaide's rooms. Part of me at first was unaccepting of the situation. Now the other part of me wanted something that I could call my own. I loved the emptiness of the West Wing, but it was a comfort when I ran into Aiden down the hall.

"Adelaide." He said, bowing to me slightly at the waist. He even put a hand behind his back.

I waited for him to straighten back up. "Oh, you do not need to be so formal." I hit him on the arm. "We are engaged, you know." I laughed, but he did not return the sentiment.

Aiden looked more mature in the few weeks he was away. He came back, not quite himself.

"Is there something the matter?" I asked him, almost afraid of the response.

Of course, there was something about the matter! He was losing his country, status as the Presidential Son, and his sleep, knowing that there would be a price on him forever - if there wasn't one already. There is a danger being in one of the most important families in history. Now, he was going to be a part of two distinguished families. He saw the weight of bearing one country's burdens and flaws on his father's shoulders. Now he was going to inherit twice the stress.

Aiden ran a finger along the decorations that littered the hallway. Most of them had been taken down, but whatever was not ruined in the attack was still hanging on this side of the palace. The planned masquerade had also been cancelled, and the invitations rescinded, just like the Rose and Thistle Charity Ball.

"Yes, and no. There are rumors I've heard. There are things that I am sure are better left unseen or unsaid." His tone was serious.

I motioned towards my room. We walked out on the balcony, where I knew we would not be disturbed.

"Where is your guard?"

"There was a high overturn of staff here. After everything that happened with those that wished me dead, many resigned their posts."

Aiden snorted. "I am shocked that one left. The dark-haired one with the blue-green eyes seemed awfully protective."

"Actually, I sent Officer Durant away. He was not one that outright resigned." I put a hand on the balcony railing and sucked in a breath. I felt Aiden's presence next to me before I saw that he stood close to me, looking out at the gardens.

"Why would you do that? It seemed like you two were close. I had heard … *rumors,* even."

I put my bandaged hand on top of his on the railing. With the photographers gone with the cancellation of the masquerade event, it seemed pointless to keep wearing gloves.

"I thought that you did not listen to rumors or read the trash that is published about us in the papers."

A smile tugged at the corners of his mouth. "I don't. I have my Secret Service members read them and they report to me a summed-up version of what is printed. Adelaide. I want to be honest with you. I think that after everything I owe you at least that much."

I moved my hand away from his and turned to face him straight-on. "All right. Go on."

Aiden ran his fingers through his sandy locks. Underneath where the sun did not hit, his head was starting to turn a light brown. I wondered how long it would take him to start greying. He looked from the gardens and then straight at me.

Whatever he was about to say could not be

good.

"I was not lying that from the moment I laid my eyes on you that I wanted you. I've loved you for a long time, as I once confessed to you. I truly did not know what our fathers would be announcing that day when our engagement was announced. It killed me that you might not have felt the same way. I knew about Prince Henri Francois a year ago. My father was angry that his alliance was going to be ruined. He trashed his study in the White House. The staff was not happy that he damaged some historically priceless relics. I saw some of the copies of your letters to one another. I had no idea how my father got hold of them. I was defeated, and I knew it. But, when months went by and there was no news of you running away with him, my father thought that maybe I would have a chance after all. Our country has been in dire need of assistance for quite some time. We are surrounded by enemies and have traitors within. The money in the government ran out a long time ago and our debts were being called in. I knew that my father was going to negotiate some kind of alliance with yours. I did not know all the details or even that they were planning on uniting our households. I just knew that if there was a chance that I could be with you, then I wanted to take it."

I opened my mouth to say something.

Aiden held up a hand. "Let me finish."

I nodded and stayed silent.

"I asked around about you. I could not figure out why you were so different. Then I discovered that your head injuries had caused some memory loss. I thought I was finally going to have a clean slate, and a fair chance of dating you. Your guard was overbearing and off-putting. I could not put my finger on it ... until he rescued you from drowning that day we were in the paddleboat. I saw that you looked at *him* the way that I wanted you to look at *me*. As soon as I heard about the attack on the palace, I knew that I could not lose you a third time. I thought I had lost you once to Prince Henri Francois. I was certain that I was losing you again, to your noble guard. Then I thought you were dead for hours. The only thing I could think about was that I never had the chance to tell you how I really felt, that I would never get to tell you that even with the memory loss and all the changes to your personality, I still loved you. In fact, I think I love you even more. There is a realness to you now, more than ever. Before, I idolized you, but now, after having gotten to know you … to know that your favorite tea is raspberry rose, and you love the color sunset red … as soon as I saw you run offstage during the statement for your safety, I arranged passage back to you."

At this point, Aiden kneeled before me. On both of his knees. He took my bandaged hand in his own. "Adelaide Whyndam, I know that this is very unconventional. I had this planned out a million other ways in my head. I know that you do not remember me much from my time spent here at Pembroke Palace. But none of that matters to me. I am willing to stake a lifetime of happiness trying to figure us out. I want to spend the next eighty years being your Prince-Consort and doing whatever you ask of me. At the end of the day, I want you and I will take any part of you that you will give me."

Aiden pulled out a box and flipped open the cover. Inside, atop the black velvet, was a little red ribbon.

"I know it isn't much, but they would not let me into the royal treasury without you present. Apparently, you are supposed to pick out your own ring."

I did not honestly know what to say.

He continued. "The ribbon is sunset red, and I hope that in the near future, we can cut it while watching the sunset, as I put on the ring you were meant to wear. Will you marry this American, who will love you endlessly?"

I took a step and went down to my knees as well. I pried his hands off the little black box and set it aside. "In this moment, I am not a princess. I am not a title higher than you. In this moment, I am just me."

Beads of sweat formed at his hairline.

For it being the end of October, the evening air was cool as the wind enveloped us in its embrace.

We were both about at the same level now. I brought my lips to his and gave him a whisper of a kiss. In this kiss, I poured the beginnings of feelings not shared, and a hopefulness not spoken.

He wrapped a hand around my waist. His other hand went to the back of my neck. He pulled me in closer.

This moment was perfect. Nothing could have ruined it.

Aiden stopped kissing me but leaned back to stare into my eyes. "So, is this a yes?"

I bit my bottom lip. "Yes, I mean. We are already engaged, but this is now a two-way street."

He trailed kisses down my neck as I leaned back on the floor of the balcony. His body was against mine as he kissed me, more slowly this time.

It was as if time itself had stopped.

Eventually, we came to our senses and stopped before things took off at a pace that they could not be stopped.

Aiden tied the little red ribbon around my ring finger. Thank goodness it was not the hand that was bandaged. Otherwise, he would have needed a longer piece.

I walked him to the door, where he gave me a quick peck before leaving to go to his own rooms. I closed the door and fell back onto my bed. I hadn't bothered to change. Instead, I blissfully fell asleep.

CHAPTER XIX

November was almost over. Aiden and I had settled on a date. We would wed on my birthday. At least, we would not have to remember too many dates; I had found out that his birthday was on New Year's Day, and I originally suggested his birthday, but I knew that everyone around us wanted the wedding to take place sooner, rather than later.

I still kept my red ribbon tied around my finger, but Aiden and I did go to the royal treasury soon after he proposed to me on my balcony. I ended up picking a large emerald surrounded by diamonds. If the rumors were to be believed, apparently my ring was once gifted to Cleopatra from Marc Antony, as a symbol of their eternal love for one another.

I was in the queen's suite, trying on my wedding dress. The train was so long that

Constance and Faith had to use the queen's room to finish their masterpiece.

"How are you feeling?" Queen Celine asked me.

I kept staring down at my ring while my maids fussed with the dress. It was going to be their best creation yet.

Queen Celine clapped her hands. "Ladies, can you give us a moment alone?"

Constance and Faith scurried out of the room faster than I could say anything.

"You do realize that they'll be back in ten minutes, right?"

Queen Celine laughed quietly. "I know how you must be feeling. I too was anxious before my big day."

"It's not that." I was wringing my hands together. I no longer needed to wear gloves or bandages. My gunshot wound was healed, but a nasty, jagged scar remained. It would remind me of Wesley every time I looked at it. I knew that he would do the same every time he looked at his own hand as well. Our wounds were a mirror reflection as the bullet scraped through our once entwined hands. "I have a desire to tell Aiden about who I really am. That he is not crazy to think that I just simply forgot about things after the first assassination."

"Attempt. It was an assassination attempt." Queen Celine said curtly. "You can never say anything, not even to your fiancé. Not until the wedding tomorrow takes place. Maybe not even then."

"What do you mean, not even then?" I stepped off the little platform I was standing on.

Queen Celine looked at me like I have never seen her look before. She looked worried. "Have you said anything to anyone at all?"

"No, I swear it. The only ones that I used to talk to were Giles and Jacinta. I've said nothing after their deaths."

"Their deaths were the hardest on me out of everyone else on that list. Jacinta was like a sister to me. We were very close, which is why I entrusted you to her care. I knew that she and Giles could not conceive children. In a way, you were my gift to her." A tear slipped from her eye. Queen Celine patted it away with the swipe of one graceful finger. "No matter. I cannot go back into the past. No one can. You are Adelaide Rosalind Isadora Elita Whyndam. Adalia does not exist. She never did. So, there is no point in telling a fictitious story about her life now. You, my darling, are the heir to this strong monarchy. You are the last of the Whyndams, as Aiden is the last of the American dynasty. Enjoy the privacy of your honeymoon while it lasts. As soon as the two of you return, you'll be expected to make an heir."

I put my hands on my hips. "Are you worried that someone would try to kill both of us?"

"No, I am worried about what marriage will mean for you. You will be in my position. I just do not want what happened eighteen years ago to happen again. It would be a shame if history repeated itself."

"Have you received any threats? I thought all of that was over with now. It seemed like everyone who resigned was either scared or possibly had a hand in the attack."

"Let us hope that tomorrow brings the people together instead of apart. You must play the part of the blushing bride and exude bridal bliss and pure happiness for the sake of peace."

"I intend to, but it will be real for me too." I said, as my maids returned. It was evident that this conversation was over.

~

There was a loud knock on my door. "Come in." I was reading a book in bed in my white satin nightgown. My maids thought it best that I looked the part of the bride for my last night as a Miss. Tomorrow I would be Aiden Smith's Mrs.

Aiden stood there in the doorway. His eyes flicked up and down as he was taking in the sight of me.

I put my book down on my nightstand. "Close the door, Aiden. You know you're not supposed to see the bride the night before the wedding."

He looked a little stunned to see me dressed down like this.

I was unsure why. I mean, he had seen me in a nightgown before, when I was in the infirmary, but I will admit that it was a little cotton thing. The way I was dressed tonight, I knew how I looked. I looked like a queen. My golden hair was curled loosely and cascaded down my back. My satin nightgown had a matching robe that had exquisite baby pearls sewn into a regal design.

Aiden's foot struck the door closed. He locked it and turned back to me. "Can I sit next to you?" He was nervous.

"Um. Not on the bed." A blush budded at the base of my neck.

Aiden took a seat on the chair of my vanity. He crossed one leg over his knee uncomfortably. "Tomorrow you will be my wife."

I already knew that.

The words seemed to impact him. The words heavy on his tongue. "Wife. Wife. Wife."

I moved from the bed and sat in his lap on the chair. I only hoped that the vanity cushion could support us both. I wrapped my arms around his neck. "I believe the proper title will be Your Majesty."

His gaze traveled down my neck.

I moved my hair off my shoulder.

He moved his mouth into the small space

between my shoulder and my neck as I cringed. My breath hitched a little. I untucked his shirt and fumbled with it, moving it over his head. He grabbed my thighs over my nightgown and lifted me up. He sat up with me and carried me over to the bed, laying me down gently.

His lips went up to my ear. A deep growl released from within my throat. I had never heard that sound before.

Aiden laughed before crashing his lips down to mine. We became a tangled mess of limbs and teeth.

After a while, Aiden pulled away. "I think I am pressing my luck. We will do this and so much more tomorrow." He whispered and drew a kiss to my forehead.

I sat up as my dress was high up my thigh and my strap was hanging off my shoulder. I could only imagine what my beautifully curled hair had looked like. I'd have to tell my maids that I had a terrible nightmare.

"Wait." I pulled him back down to the bed. "I want you to stay."

The grin was back. His smile contagiously spreading from ear to ear.

"Not like that! We have tomorrow night for that. I meant that I want you to hold me. I want you to stay because you want to and not because of husbandly duty. Not because I am the princess or any of that. But because you want to."

Aiden blew out the candles by my nightstand and crawled beneath the covers. "That's all I've ever wanted."

I kissed him on the cheek and laid my head on his shoulder.

We fell asleep soundly. Him listening to my breathing and me to the beat of his loving heart for me. I knew that a name did not matter. Aiden had fallen in love with me; Adalia.

CHAPTER XX

I awoke to an empty bed. Aiden had slipped out in the early hours of the morning to not be seen. Even though nothing had happened last night, it would still be frowned upon if he were caught in my bed.

The side of the bed where he slept was made up now. A single red dahlia lay on the pillow with a note. Sunset red. How perfect. I picked up the flower and held it to my nose, breathing in the floral scent. I set it down on my nightstand and tore open the letter.

Your very life depends on you __NOT__ entering the cathedral today. Absence makes the heart grow fonder. Consequences be cursed.

A. R. I. E

ARIE? Who was Arie? I ignored the ominous warning and tossed it into the coals of the fireplace. Nothing was going to ruin today. It was my wedding, after all.

The dress was exquisite, made of silk, satin, and lace. I moved with such glittering grace as the stitched-in gems dazzled in the light. To Queen Celine's dismay, I refused to wear one of her tiaras. Faith instead weaved a crown of white orchids into my up-do hairstyle. Today, of all days, I wanted to have something of myself, something that made me feel like I was still back at the country estate, like Aiden and I would have found each other even then—even if Adelaide were still alive, and I were never summoned to Pembroke Palace. My crown of flowers would be the one thing that I could call my own. It made me Adalia. It made me who I was, and on all the days of my life, I wanted to be me on my wedding day. At least, one last time.

It was finally the moment in which I would meet my husband and Prince-Consort-to-Be. At the altar, I kept staring at him. He looked dashing in a black suit. A red-and-white rose hung from his lapel. As I walked closer to join him at the front, I noticed the bright blue stitching that had gone into his suit. A design of budding blue roses had been hand-embroidered at his wrists. It was a nice touch of our country's symbols, intertwining at last.

There was a whole crowd of people I did not recognize. I assumed that the left was meant to be for the bride and the right side for the groom. No matter how many people I did not know, it needn't matter. They were all here bearing witness, and I knew that I had at least some people's support.

Aiden tilted towards me. "You look stunning. Absolutely breathtaking."

I blinked away small tears. I didn't want to

ruin my makeup after how effortlessly my maids worked at it.

Aiden grabbed my hand in his as we faced the archbishop presiding over us together.

"Will you, Aiden Valentine Smith, take Princess Adelaide Rosalind Isadora Elita Whyndam, to be your wedded wife?"

Aiden ran his fingers over my emerald engagement ring softly, staring into my eyes. "I will."

The archbishop looked at me now and repeated it again but changed the names around. "Do you, Princess Adelaide Rosalind Isadora Elita Whyndam..."

I drowned out the archbishop's words. ARIE. That name. It was my name. It was the first letter of the four initials of my name. I looked around the room.

Aiden squeezed my hand.

"Do you, your Highness?" The archbishop asked.

"I do. I will." I smiled back at Aiden.

He looked like he was going to faint. I felt like I was going to faint.

The archbishop nodded. "Who here does not

wish for this couple to be wedded in holy matrimony? Speak now or forever hold your peace."

The cathedral was dead silent.

Until…

"Pardon me, but this wedding is unlawful and cannot continue." A familiar male voice echoed.

Aiden and I whirled around to look behind us.

Prince Henri Francois shimmied his way down the center aisle. He threw a red dahlia on the ground.

The flower. The red dahlia on my pillowcase this morning.

It was the flower of betrayal and deceit.

Instead of looking our way, he was staring at the back of the church. He fell down to one knee, and a hand crossed over his heart.

All of a sudden, the doors burst open. An attractive young lady walked up the aisle. Her face was shrouded by sunglasses and a floppy hat. The kind one would wear to the beach. As she approached the front, I could see clearly now that her arms and legs were scattered with thick scars.

By the time this woman peeled back her hat and lowered her sunglasses, I knew who it was immediately.

I heard my voice, but I knew it was not my own.

She announced in a loud, confident tone. "I, Princess Adelaide Rosalind Isadora Elita Whyndam, do *not* agree to this marriage, and *she* is an imposter!"

Everyone's heads in the cathedral all turned from her to me.

Even Aiden dropped my hand and stepped away from me.

The cameramen swiveled their cameras towards me, wanting to catch the words I would say next.

What was there to say? I realized the entire world was watching us in this moment. The king and queen were staring, as shocked as everyone else.

I knew the cameras were zeroed in on my face and that every news station would record this moment.

I only wished that I had told Aiden the truth sooner. My eyes searched for him, but he had already left my side.

I was alone in this.

I smiled into the camera lens and spoke.

"She is correct. I am not who I have claimed to be for the last few months. I am the twin. Adelaide was always the heir. I was called to the palace upon what we all believed was her death. I am the spare. Nothing more." I paused, letting everyone absorb what I was about to say next.

I was not afraid of who I was anymore. "My name is Adalia Whyndam."

When I was finished, I looked down.

Prince Henri Francois was beside Adelaide, his arm slung around her shoulders.

The *true* Adelaide. She stared up at me from behind her sunglasses, perched on the bridge of her nose. "Hello, sister."

BOOK TWO

Sister Scandal

Shanelle Goldiene

ARRIVING IN 2022

ABOUT THE AUTHOR

Shanelle Goldiene is a true Michigander, living in the mitten all her life. She loves to read, drinks way too much tea from her fancy Vintage Jewel China set, and has been writing ever since she could hold a quill pen. Although she may not be royalty, she and her husband own land in Scotland and is a titled Lady. *Royal Reversal* is her debut novel.

If you enjoyed this book, then please let her know by leaving a review.

ACKNOWLEDGEMENTS

Thank you so much for picking up this book and staying with me on this journey all the way to the end!!! I truly appreciate you reading my first book, more than you could know.

First and foremost, I give thanks to God for giving me the ability to write and for all of my gifts and talents. Without my faith in Him, nothing would be possible.

To Dylan, my loving husband: You were the first person to read my debut novel from start to finish. You gave me the encouragement I needed to see this through to publishing. I cannot thank you enough for how lucky I am to be your wife. I love you forever and always.

To my mom, Cynthia: Thank you for believing in me as an author, and know that there is no stronger bond between that of a mother and her daughter. You have been there for me through everything in my life and I am so grateful to you. M and M forever.

Last but not least, to my editors Aimee and Abbey: Thank you from the bottom of my heart for all of your hard work. Your expert skills in grammar and content allowed me to complete my first novel.

www.ingramcontent.com/pod-product-compliance
Lightning Source LLC
Chambersburg PA
CBHW021034130626
46552CB00005B/1836